DEATH AT PORTHCURNO COVE

SALLY RIGBY

Storm
PUBLISHING

Ebook ISBN: 978-1-80508-634-5
Paperback ISBN: 978-1-80508-636-9

Cover design: Lisa Horton
Cover images: Trevillion, Shutterstock

Published by Storm Publishing.
For further information, visit:
www.stormpublishing.co

ALSO BY SALLY RIGBY

A Cornwall Murder Mystery

The Lost Girls of Penzance

The Hidden Graves of St Ives

Murder at Land's End

The Camborne Killings

Cavendish & Walker Series

Deadly Games

Fatal Justice

Death Track

Lethal Secret

Last Breath

Final Verdict

Ritual Demise

Mortal Remains

Silent Graves

Kill Shot

Dark Secrets

Broken Screams

Death's Shadow

Detective Sebastian Clifford Series

Web of Lies

Speak No Evil

This book is dedicated to my mum.

PROLOGUE

Love conquers all. That's what people say.

Yeah, right.

Well, not in my world.

I stare at the photograph in my hand and my vision blurs as I blink hard, and anger claws at my chest.

Look at them.

The perfect couple.

Her radiant smile.

His adoring gaze.

It makes me want to vomit.

The photo's edges are frayed from endless hours of restless handling. Every detail is burnt on my mind... the harsh sunlight glinting off her hair; his arm slung possessively over her shoulders; their hands locked together like they're inseparable. It's an image I can't shake, no matter how hard I try.

I throw the photo to one side and grab the half-empty beer bottle from the floor next to the bed. The bitter liquid burns as I knock it back, leaving a trail of heat in its wake. It's a familiar comfort, dulling the edges of my thoughts.

But it can't drown out the pain in my head. That's never going to go. Not now. I know that for sure.

My mobile rings but I ignore it because I'm in no mood to speak to anyone. All that matters now is formulating my plan.

They don't deserve to be happy. Not while I'm drowning in misery.

It wasn't supposed to be like this. I was convinced that we had a connection... a shared future.

How wrong could I be?

I'm such a fool.

I squeeze my eyes shut, remembering when I first saw them together. Talk about being blindsided. I never saw it coming. There were no signs. If there had been I'd have sorted it. Stopped the whole thing before it kicked off. Because I could have.

Now all I see in my mind are their intimate touches... their secret smiles when they think no one's looking... their silent communications in a language only they understand.

My stomach churns at the memories and bile rises in my throat.

Why can't I have that happiness?

It's all I've ever wanted.

I deserve to be happy.

But life's cruel. It's a merciless architect of my misery.

I'll never get what I want because someone out there has decided I'm not good enough.

The burden of injustice presses down on me.

Suffocating.

I crave release from this torment, but simple solutions seem inadequate. I need something more... something final.

I drag myself to the laptop, desperate for answers, and my fingers race across the keyboard searching for inspiration.

How to build a bomb

Where to buy a gun

What's the perfect poison

Hours pass in a blur of increasingly dark web pages and my eyes burn from the screen's harsh glow, but I can't stop. Won't stop... Until I've found the answer.

Slowly, a plan begins to take shape. It will be clean and efficient. They'll never see it coming.

I can't help but smirk.

Soon, the pain will end. For all of us.

My head throbs. A combination of too much alcohol and too little sleep. But my mind is clearer than it's been in days.

I stumble to the bathroom, barely recognising the gaunt person staring back at me in the mirror. Dark circles ring my bloodshot eyes and my skin is pale and drawn.

When did I become this hollow shell?

I splash cold water on my face, trying to wash away the lingering cobwebs of doubt. This is the only way. They've left me no choice.

The weight of what I'm about to do settles heavily on my shoulders but there's no turning back. The decision's been made.

They made their choice. Now it's time to face the consequences.

I imagine their final moments.

Will they be afraid?

Will they beg for mercy?

Or will it be over before they even realise what's happening?

I gather my supplies and a strange sense of peace washes over me.

This is it. The point of no return. Soon everything will change.

For them.

For me.

For everyone.

ONE

SUNDAY 10 SEPTEMBER

Detective Inspector Lauren Pengelly breathed in the crisp sea air, savouring the salty tang that filled her lungs. A perfect way to relax. The early morning Cornish breeze tousled her hair as she walked her two border collies down the steps towards Porthcurno's sandy beach. She'd purposely got up early and driven to the jaw-dropping, beautiful cove, wanting to make sure she'd avoid the holidaymakers who were invariably noisy with their beach games. The height of the season was over but there were still some stragglers remaining even though school holidays had ended.

Tourism might have been the life blood of Cornwall, but that didn't stop her impatience for the *silly season* to be over and for life to get back to normal. It was certainly a double-edged sword and she suspected most of the locals would agree that tourists were to be endured and not eagerly anticipated.

They reached the bottom of the steps and walked onto the pale sand. Lauren's keen eye caught some movement in the water and she squinted, making out a lone swimmer who was braving the chilly September sea.

'Rather you than me,' she murmured, giving an involuntary shiver, as her lips quirked into a half-smile.

Other than that, the beach was deserted. Exactly as she liked it. The sun was beginning to rise, and it cast a golden hue over the rugged cliffs. After a few minutes Lauren jogged across the soft golden sand until she was standing at the water's edge. The tide was coming in and it brushed against her trainers. The temptation to go for a swim in the translucent turquoise waters was strong, but she knew it would be freezing cold, despite it looking so inviting. Not to mention that she hadn't brought her wetsuit. She'd have to be content with watching.

Glancing around the perimeter of the small cove, a frown creased her brow when she couldn't see Ben and Tia. Where were they? That was weird. They'd been playing catch a moment ago with a couple of old tennis balls that she'd been throwing for each of them – until she'd been distracted by the swimmer. Unease began to wash over her but she dismissed it. She hadn't searched for them properly, that was all.

Porthcurno was her favourite of all the Cornish beaches in the area, and that was no mean feat. It was idyllic, although small, surrounded by rocks, and accessed from the road via a short walk down the steps. The cliffs loomed over her, their shadows casting long, eerie shapes on the sand. Surely her dogs hadn't run away. No, they couldn't have done, she told herself. They knew better than to do that. They were exceptionally well trained – everyone said so. People were always stopping her to comment on their behaviour. Something must have distracted them, but if that was the case, surely they would have barked to catch her attention. That's what they always did... well, usually.

So where were they?

Lauren turned and headed away from the water's edge, desperately scanning the area for any sign of her dogs.

What if they'd been stolen? No... that was crazy; it couldn't have happened without her noticing. She'd only been distracted for a minute, if that, and there had been no other people on the beach at the time.

'Ben, Tia. Where are you?' she shouted, her voice carrying in the wind. Hopefully they hadn't found a dead seal or something equally unpleasant.

'Ben, Tia,' she called again, but there was still no response. Whatever it was, they were fully engrossed.

Suddenly she caught sight of a wagging tail in the distance, near one of the small caves that dotted the base of the cliffs, and she breathed a sigh of relief. The natural caves often served as impromptu shelters for beachgoers, although at this early hour, they should have been empty.

'What have you two found?' she shouted while running over.

As she reached them, her breath caught in her throat. The dogs were sniffing two people who were on a blanket and lying haphazardly against the rocks, their arms and legs twisted in unnatural positions. Vacant expressions covered their faces and lifeless eyes stared blankly ahead.

They were dead.

Her heart began pumping wildly in her chest.

'Bloody hell,' she muttered, taking in the scene.

The couple appeared to be in their early twenties. The young woman was dressed in a short denim skirt and a white T-shirt, with a cerise pink glittery cardigan draped over her slender shoulders. Her blonde hair hung loosely, framing her face. The guy, whose hair was as curly as hers was straight, wore dark shorts and a striped T-shirt.

What the hell happened for their lives to be so abruptly ended?

Who were they? Locals? Tourists? She'd have to call it in, but first she needed to get the dogs away before they contaminated the scene further.

'Ben. Tia. Come,' she called sternly, her voice slicing

through the eerie silence. The dogs immediately turned around and obediently trotted towards her.

'Follow me,' she urged, taking them away from the small cave and onto the main beach.

The dogs obeyed and when they were well away from the scene she knelt down, stroking their heads to reassure them. 'Sit and stay,' she ordered, giving them a single wag of the finger. It was a gesture they were familiar with and they knew what to do.

Lauren took out a pair of disposable gloves from her pocket and pulled them on before heading back to where the bodies were situated, making sure not to disturb anything. There was a prosecco bottle lying on its side and, next to it, an empty black, heart-shaped ring box lined with lilac crushed velvet.

She noticed the woman's left hand. A diamond and sapphire ring sparkled on her engagement finger. It looked new.

Peering a little closer, she caught sight of a handwritten note lying next to the young man. She took a step to the side so she could see it more clearly. But all that was written was 'SORRY' in black ink and in capital letters.

Who were they saying sorry to?

Their families?

Their friends?

Each other?

A chill ran down her spine and a wave of nausea washed over her but she breathed through it, knowing that she had to stay composed.

She turned her back on the distressing scene and, after sucking in a long breath, pulled out her mobile from a pocket in her jeans and keyed in the number for the station.

'Penzance police,' the voice answered.

'Good morning, Sergeant Ford,' she said recognising the gravelly voice of the officer who often worked on the front desk. 'It's DI Pengelly here, I'm phoning in an incident.'

'Morning, ma'am. What can you tell me?' he asked briskly.

'I was walking my dogs on Porthcurno Beach this morning and came across two bodies. One male and one female. Please call the pathologist and also send out officers to secure the scene. I suggest at least four in order to keep the area safe from all sides. I'll wait here until they arrive to ensure nothing is disturbed.'

'Will do, ma'am. Can you ascertain the circumstances of the deaths from what you've seen so far?'

'I can't be sure, Sergeant, but it's pointing to a double suicide. The pathologist will confirm.'

She ended the call and pressed speed dial for her detective sergeant, Matt Price.

'Morning, ma'am,' Matt greeted, answering after only one ring, hesitation in his voice, as if he was expecting to hear the worst.

'Sorry to call you so early, Matt. I need you at Porthcurno Beach. I was out walking the dogs this morning and came across a young couple who appeared to have taken their own lives.'

Matt let out a low whistle. 'Oh no, that's dreadful, ma'am. What on earth could have been so bad for them to do that? Rhetorical question,' he hurriedly added. 'Can you give me any more details?'

Lauren took a deep breath, reliving the scene in her mind. 'It was the dogs who discovered the bodies, not me. But luckily they don't appear to have damaged the scene. They were just sniffing. The couple are lying against the rocks in a small cave towards the rear of the beach. They looked barely out of their teens. There was a prosecco bottle lying on its side next to a small jewellery box. The girl was wearing an engagement ring that appeared to be new judging by the way it sparkled in the sun.'

'An engagement ring? So the man proposed and then they took their own lives. That seems a bit weird, don't you think?'

'My sentiments exactly,' Lauren agreed. 'But there was a note next to the young man on which was simply written, "Sorry", which implies that's what it was. It doesn't make sense, for sure. But then we never get a clear-cut death... there's always something...' Her words fell away.

'I'm surprised they were still there; wouldn't the tide have washed them out to sea?' Matt asked, sounding puzzled.

'Probably more by luck than judgement. They were quite a way up the beach and the water, even at high tide, doesn't go that far. Thank goodness, because otherwise we wouldn't have known they were dead until their bodies washed up on the shore somewhere. That's if they ever did.'

'Did you check them for identification?'

'I didn't want to compromise the area any more than necessary so didn't look. I'm waiting for the pathologist. I believe Henry's on duty today, thank goodness. We'll discuss this further when you arrive,' she said, wanting to end their conversation or it would delay things even further.

'Yes, ma'am. I'll be with you as soon as I can. Are the dogs okay after their ordeal... If we can call it that?'

'Yes, they're fine, sitting quietly next to me. They'll need to go home at some point, preferably sooner rather than later but I won't do anything until the pathologist arrives. Sorry for disturbing your day off. Had you anything planned?'

Why was she engaging in further conversation when she'd told him to get moving? She shook her head.

'Household chores and I'd promised to take Dani out to the play equipment after lunch,' Matt answered, referring to his three-year-old daughter, for whom Lauren had a soft spot ever since she'd rescued the toddler from a kidnapper who'd been targeting children at local nurseries.

'Send her my apologies,' she said before ending the call and replacing the phone in her pocket.

Lauren moved further up the beach, settling near the steps.

She leant against the rocks, keeping the dogs close but allowing them to play. Her eyes darted between the ocean and the small cove concealing the grim scene, unable to shake from her mind the image of the young couple's lifeless bodies.

Lauren's gut twisted with a familiar dread... something about the scene felt off.

Who were they and what desperate circumstances had led them here?

Was there more to this story than met the eye?

A chill ran down her spine, and it wasn't the sea breeze. In her years on the force, Lauren had learnt to trust her instincts. And they were screaming that this was no simple suicide pact.

She glanced up the steps, willing the requested officers to arrive.

Whatever secrets this beach held, Lauren knew with certainty this was only the beginning.

TWO

Matt arrived at Porthcurno and parked behind Lauren's Audi, close to the steps leading down to the beach. Peering in his rearview mirror, he noticed another car pulling into the car park, stopping a few metres away. It was Henry Carpenter, the pathologist.

After taking off his seatbelt, Matt left the car and made a beeline for the man. The cool morning breeze brushed against his skin and he shivered, pulling his jacket around him. He'd been in Cornwall for over nine months but the chill beside the ocean still surprised him.

'This doesn't sound too good,' Matt said when he reached Henry, his voice tinged with apprehension.

'I know. A young couple,' Henry responded, his expression bleak.

A person would be forgiven if, at first glance, they thought Henry was a bumbling older man, but appearances were deceptive. The pathologist was as sharp as they came, and excellent at his job. Lauren would be relieved he'd been allocated the case. Although Henry was thorough, he wasn't precious over his findings, unlike others. He was cognisant of their need to know how a person died as soon as possible, even if the official report hadn't been written.

'Barely out of their teens, according to the DI. She suspects they took their own lives, because of a note that had been left,' Matt replied, exhaling deeply. 'What on earth could have happened for them to do that in such a manner?'

'Unfortunately, suicides happen more often than people realise,' Henry said, shaking his head. 'Only the other day, I was reading a research paper on the number of suicides among young people and how they're on the increase in the UK. North America, too.'

'Did the paper offer any explanations for this trend?' Matt asked, his voice heavy and his shoulders slumped.

'They went into probable causes, and found a range of contributory factors. But irrespective of this increase, it's still dreadful for all concerned when faced with it.' Henry's jaw tightened and his fingers drummed an agitated rhythm on the roof of his car.

'Let's head to the scene,' Matt said, uneasiness settling in his chest.

Henry opened the back door of his car and pulled out the worn brown bag he always carried whenever called out to a crime scene.

Side by side, they walked in silence down the first set of steps to the beach until reaching the area that had already been cordoned off. Matt signed himself and Henry in, before continuing down the remainder of the steps. Reaching the bottom, Matt was struck by the beautiful scene in front of him. Porthcurno was one of the most picturesque beaches in the area, and he'd been there several times with his family. Yet, he knew what they were about to face would be anything but *beautiful*.

Matt took a deep breath as they approached the scene. Even after years on the job, facing death never got easier. He was known among his colleagues for his sensitivity to gruesome sights, and he silently hoped this scene wouldn't be too graphic. If there was any blood all bets were off as to whether he'd be able to view the body without vomiting.

The sound of the waves crashing against the shore seemed at odds with the stark reality they were about to uncover. Questions raced through Matt's mind. What had led this young couple to such a tragic end? Was it a planned act or a moment of desperation?

Matt caught Henry's eye and a look of understanding passed between them... both seasoned professionals, yet still affected by the human cost of their work.

Lauren stood to the left, Ben and Tia lying quietly at her feet. She seemed composed, but Matt noticed the subtle tension in her posture. Matt nodded to her in acknowledgement, ready to begin the awful task ahead.

'Morning, ma'am,' Matt said, trying to keep his tone steady.

'Inspector,' Henry added with a nod.

'Morning to you, too,' Lauren replied. She turned to the dogs. 'Stay.'

Lauren led Matt and Henry towards one of the small rock formations. The air was cooler in the shade, and the smell of the ocean strong.

The young couple's lifeless bodies looked almost peaceful, and if it wasn't for their awkward positioning Matt would have assumed that they'd simply fallen asleep.

'As you can see from the glasses and bottle, they've most likely had a drink. There's a ring box on the ground and what appears to be a new ring on the left ring finger of the female victim.'

'Why get engaged before taking your life? You don't think they could have died of hypothermia, do you?' Matt looked at Henry, hoping for a simple explanation, but not really expecting one.

'It hasn't been cold enough,' Henry replied, with a wave of

his hand. 'But obviously, that's something to be investigated once I have them at the morgue. Judging by their pallor, though, it's extremely unlikely.'

Henry pulled on his coveralls, gloved up and then took a step forward, crouching down by the bodies, his camera in hand.

'So young,' Matt said, a deep sadness settling in him. 'Do you think it could be a suicide pact? Can you tell yet how they died?'

'Patience, young man,' Henry said, glancing up at him. 'There's some corneal clouding in their eyes, which could indicate a drug overdose, but that can occur post mortem for a number of reasons, which we'll find out after my investigation is complete.'

'What if it was accidental?' Matt suggested, his voice low. 'They could have come here to celebrate their engagement, had some prosecco, and then...' He hesitated, choosing his words carefully. 'Maybe they took something else, not realising how it would interact with the alcohol.'

Matt left the implication hanging in the air. The idea of an accident, rather than a deliberate act, felt marginally less tragic. But as he glanced at the still forms on the beach, he knew that regardless of how it happened, the impact on their families would be devastating.

Lauren nodded. 'It's possible. We can't rule anything out at this stage. But let's not get ahead of ourselves. We need facts, not speculation.'

'Certainly that's an option to consider,' Henry said. 'We won't know anything for certain until I've completed the post-mortems.'

'Is the bottle empty?' Matt asked, nodding at it.

Henry took a photo of it in situ and then picked it up, peering in and giving it a shake. 'Yes.'

'So half a bottle each, plus some drugs... They would have been well out of it,' Matt said.

'Stop with the supposition and let me do my job,' Henry said, but not unkindly.

'Sorry,' Matt said, glancing down at his feet.

'Henry, can you check for ID, please?' Lauren asked. 'We need to inform next of kin.'

On the sand, beside the girl's body, was a cream straw bag, with a thin brown leather strap. Henry opened it carefully and unzipped a side pocket. He pulled out a driving licence. 'Jasmine Dodd, age twenty-one,' he said, stating the information in a matter-of-fact voice. 'According to this she lives at Rosehill Gardens, Heamoor, Penzance.'

'Thanks, Henry. I know the area. And the young man?' Lauren asked.

Henry checked the man's pockets, finding a driving licence. 'Finley Glenister. Also twenty-one. He lives at Alverton Road.' The pathologist carefully replaced the licence, his usual clinical demeanour slipping for a moment. 'Such a waste,' he murmured.

'We'll get to the bottom of this. For them and their families,' Matt said quietly, more to himself than anyone else, knowing that every detail would be crucial in uncovering the truth behind this heartbreaking scene.

'I agree,' Lauren said, a determined expression on her face. 'Thanks, Henry. Before we go, have you noticed anything else that might assist in the investigation?'

'Not yet. The fact there's a note supports our initial suspicion that it was a double suicide, but the postmortem will confirm it. I'll contact you the moment there's anything to add.'

'Okay, thanks, Henry. Come on, Matt,' Lauren said with a resigned sigh. 'We have families to contact and it's not going to be easy.'

'What about the dogs, ma'am?' Matt asked, glancing at Ben

and Tia, who were lying on the sand patiently, their eyes glued on Lauren.

'Of course. I forgot for a moment. Follow me to my house. Once I've settled the dogs, which will only take a few minutes, we'll visit the families. In the meantime, contact the office so we can get started on discovering more about the victims. Do you know who's in today?'

'Ellie and Billy,' Matt replied, referring to Detective Constables Naylor and Ward.

'Call Ellie while I'm dealing with the dogs. By the way, are they still seeing each other?'

Ellie, Matt's ex-colleague from Lenchester who'd been visiting on holiday and had ended up being seconded to them while Tamsin was on sick leave recovering from a broken leg, had struck up a friendship with Billy. Well... more than a friendship. How Billy would react when Ellie returned to Lenchester was anyone's guess.

'I believe so, ma'am. But they're careful not to bring it into work, so to speak.'

'Good. That's as it should be.' Lauren turned to the dogs. 'Ben, Tia. Come.'

Once the dogs had come over, they headed up the steps towards their cars.

'What were you planning to do today?' Lauren asked, sounding as if she was trying to make small talk to lighten the heavy mood.

'You've already asked that, ma'am,' Matt said with a smile as he ran a hand through his hair. 'Cleaning this morning... Mum's on one of her sprees. This afternoon we'd planned to take Dani to the park.' He paused, glancing towards the beach. 'We'd talked about coming here if the weather was nice.'

His boss nodded, as if understanding the unspoken implication. The beach, usually a place of relaxation, was now a crime scene.

'Sorry, too much on my mind. I'd forgotten I'd asked. But I'm sure your family understands,' Lauren said, her tone sympathetic but professional. 'This job rarely keeps sociable hours.'

'You're right about that, ma'am,' he replied with a sigh.

Matt returned to his car and waited while Lauren secured the dogs and then drove out of the car park behind her. His thoughts dwelled on the tragic scene they'd left behind and the impact it was going to have on everyone involved in the couple's lives. It was hard to fathom the desperation that had led them to such a decision.

Once they'd reached Lauren's house, a late Victorian town house in the centre of St Just, Matt pulled out his phone and called Ellie.

'Hi, Matt,' she answered breezily. 'You're calling early.'

'I'm with the DI. We have two bodies on Porthcurno Beach. It looks like they've taken their own lives but we don't know yet for sure. We're going to visit the families. We've identified them as Jasmine Dodd, who lives in Rosehill Gardens, and Finley Glenister from Alverton Road. Both aged twenty-one.'

'That's awful,' Ellie gasped.

'Yeah. I want you to confirm the addresses are correct and find out who they live with, please. Text me as soon as you know. The DI will be a few more minutes while she sorts out the dogs. She was the one to find the bodies.'

'Oh my goodness, what a shock that must have been.'

'It was Ben and Tia who actually located them. They don't appear at all bothered by it. But then why would they.'

'I'll be as quick as I can,' Ellie said.

Matt ended the call, and his thoughts drifted to the task ahead.

Informing families that a loved one had died was the part of his job he dreaded most. Finding the right words was never easy, especially knowing that nothing could truly ease the pain of such a loss.

He glanced up and saw Lauren hurrying towards him. She'd changed out of her casual leggings and T-shirt and was now wearing a dark grey trouser suit and pale pink shirt. She headed to his car, opened the door and slipped inside, pulling over the seatbelt and clicking it in place in one smooth move.

'Let's get this over with,' she said with a heavy sigh. 'We'll go to Jasmine's family first.'

THREE

SUNDAY 10 SEPTEMBER

'According to Ellie, Jasmine Dodd's an only child and she's currently studying at Southampton University,' Matt said once they'd pulled up outside the terraced house where the victim lived, and he'd checked his phone, appreciating the detail the officer had provided in such a short space of time. 'Finley Glenister is also studying there. He has a younger sister called Faith.'

The narrow street was lined with similar grey, pebbled-dashed houses, each with small, paved parking areas out the front.

'An only child,' Lauren said, exhaling slowly, but saying nothing further.

She didn't need to. Losing a child was beyond the imagination of most people. But when that child was the only one, in Matt's experience, that often left parents with very little desire to continue going on with their lives. He shuddered at the thought.

They exited the car and walked up to the door, which was straddled by two large pots each containing blossoming pink and red fuchsias. Matt knocked firmly and glanced at the small garden area. Brightly coloured purple and white agapanthus were situated under the window leaning against the dark fence, hiding much of the moss which was streaked along the bottom. The family obviously loved their garden.

After only a few seconds, a petite woman with short grey hair answered, her brow furrowed as she took in the sight of the two detectives.

'Mrs Dodd?' Lauren asked.

'Yes,' the woman replied, her voice trembling slightly.

'I'm Detective Inspector Pengelly, and this is Detective Sergeant Price,' Lauren said while holding out her warrant card. 'May we come in for a moment, please?'

'What's it about?' Mrs Dodd said, taking a cursory glance at the ID Lauren was proffering. The woman's voice wavered, and her eyes darted between the two detectives.

'We'd rather talk to you inside,' Lauren said softly.

The woman opened the door, allowing them to enter her home. The hallway was narrow, lined with family photos and a faint scent of lavender. The house appeared impeccably tidy.

'Are you alone?' Matt asked, keeping his voice steady so as not to alert the woman until they had explained why they were there.

'My husband, Adrian, is here. We were talking about whether to phone you because Jasmine didn't come home last night. I went into her bedroom at nine to see if she had any washing and saw that her bed hadn't been slept in. I was totally shocked because she always tells us if she's not coming home. Adrian said to call but I thought you had to wait for twenty-four hours before raising the alarm.' Mrs Dodd's voice broke slightly, and she swallowed hard.

Interesting that calling the police was their first thought, and not contacting Finley or his family. Matt filed that detail away for later consideration. Right now, they had a more difficult task ahead.

'Where's Mr Dodd?' Lauren enquired.

'In the kitchen. Would you like to speak to both of us?' Mrs Dodd asked, biting down on her bottom lip.

'Yes, if we may,' Lauren confirmed.

'Okay.' She turned her head away from them until she was facing the rear of the house. 'Adrian, the police are here.'

Within a few seconds, a tall man with closely cropped grey hair hurried out from the room at the end of the corridor. Concern shone from his eyes.

'What is it? Is it Jasmine?' he asked, not even attempting to hide the fear and dread he appeared to be feeling. 'It is, isn't it? I told you we should contact the police straight away,' he said in an accusatory manner, glaring at his wife.

'We'd like to speak to you both. Let's go into the lounge,' Lauren suggested, keeping her tone even and gesturing towards a door to their right. 'Is it through here?'

'Tell us now. What is it?' the man demanded, his voice rising.

Matt glanced at Lauren. Wherever they imparted the news, it really wasn't going to make any difference.

'We're really sorry to tell you that this morning Jasmine was found on Porthcurno Beach,' Lauren said, her voice weighted with care.

Mr Dodd's face drained of colour, his eyes widening in disbelief. 'What do you mean "found"?' he asked, his voice barely above a whisper.

'Jasmine's dead. We're very sorry for your loss,' Lauren said.

A choke escaped Mrs Dodd. 'How? What happened? Where was Finley?'

Was she going to tell them?

'All I can say is that Jasmine wasn't alone.' Lauren paused, allowing her words to sink in. 'We can't divulge the name of the person she was with until the family has been informed. Please, let's sit down and we'll explain everything we know,' Lauren said in a low voice.

'But this other person is dead, too,' Mrs Dodd pushed.

Lauren nodded.

'It's Finley, isn't it?'

'We can't confirm that,' Lauren answered.

'You don't have to; it's written all over your faces.'

Lauren glanced at Matt and he shrugged. There was no point in denying it now.

'Mrs Dodd—'

'We'll go in here,' Mr Dodd said, interrupting Lauren and turning to the right.

They followed him into a small lounge, where the decor was cosy and welcoming, with soft, cushioned furniture and tall lamps. The family photos on the walls seemed to radiate happier times.

'Tell us what happened,' Mr Dodd demanded once they were all seated.

He was perched rigidly, as if his spine had been replaced by an iron rod.

'The pathologist is undertaking a postmortem at the moment,' Matt explained, choosing his words carefully. 'But there was a note found next to them, on which was written the word "sorry".'

'Are you... are you saying that it was suicide?' Mr Dodd's face twisted in confusion and disbelief.

'That can't be right,' Mrs Dodd exclaimed. 'Jasmine wouldn't do that. She wouldn't. I know that for sure. She was very happy. You know she's very clever. She's been planning to study for her master's after she'd finished her third year. She's the first person in our family to go to university and...' A single sob escaped her lips and she leant forward and wrapped her arms around her legs. 'You're wrong... You must be wrong. Are you sure it was her? Our Jasmine. Are you sure?' A low guttural groan escaped her lips.

'Yes, we are, Mrs Dodd. We've seen her driving licence. I'm so very sorry,' Lauren replied softly.

The woman wailed and then started sobbing uncontrollably, her whole body shaking. Mr Dodd, who was sitting next to her on the sofa, put his arm around her shoulders and pulled her close to him, his own eyes brimming with tears.

Matt's insides clenched. Delivering news like this was always the hardest part of the job. He'd never get used to it. Never.

'We're so very sorry for your loss,' Lauren repeated. 'But right now we're trying to find out what happened to Jasmine and we really need your help.'

'But... but... you think it was... was... suicide,' Mr Dodd said, his voice trembling.

'Like I said, we're waiting to hear back from the pathologist but it's certainly likely that they took their own lives,' Matt repeated. 'Because of the note.'

'Do you know who wrote it?' Mr Dodd asked.

'Not yet. It was all in capital letters.'

'Their writing is very different. Finley had beautiful writing, but Jasmine's was often illegible and not at all neat. We used to joke that she should have been a doctor...' His voice faded away, and his eyes glazed over.

'The pathology department will take a look at the note,' Matt said. 'We did notice that they had been celebrating with glasses of prosecco. Next to Jasmine on the sand was a small jewellery box, and she was wearing a ring on her engagement finger.'

'Did you know they were planning to get engaged?' Lauren asked, staring directly at the grieving parents.

Mrs Dodd glanced up at Lauren, blinking, but not speaking, while Mr Dodd shook his head.

'We didn't, but they've been going out for a long time, and we thought it might happen at some time,' Mr Dodd answered, his voice heavy with sorrow. 'They've known each other since school and began dating when they were seventeen. They went to Southampton University together, too.'

'We haven't yet informed Finley's parents about what has happened, so please could you keep this to yourselves until they know?' Lauren asked.

'Oh, yes, of course,' Mr Dodd replied. 'How will we know when that will be?'

'We're going to see them immediately after we've left you. But before we go, we do have a few more questions about Jasmine, if that's okay?' Lauren asked, directing her question at Mr rather than Mrs Dodd, who was staring at the floor and no longer engaging with them.

'Yes.' Mr Dodd sounded stoic, but Matt suspected he was likely to break down at any moment.

'You mentioned Jasmine being at university, and I take it she was home for the summer. Is that correct?' Lauren asked.

Mrs Dodd glanced at them and sat up straighter. 'Yes, she's been home all summer. She always spends her holidays here and works at a local supermarket to save up for term time. We can't afford to help her out much, not like Finley's parents... They're rich. She also has a student loan.'

The woman spoke as if Jasmine was still alive. It would take a long time for that to change. At least that's what happened with Matt's wife, Leigh. Even now he occasionally talked about her in the present tense and not the past.

'What was Jasmine studying?' Lauren asked.

'Sociology. She took it at A level and loved it so much she wanted to study it further,' Mrs Dodd explained.

'Were you happy with her choice?' Lauren asked.

'Us?' Mrs Dodd asked, sounding surprised at the question. 'Why would we get involved? She's the clever one and knows what's best. We don't know anything about university, do we, Adrian?'

Mr Dodd shook his head. 'No. We were happy for her to study whatever she wanted as long as she enjoyed it.'

'Did Finley take the same course as Jasmine?' Lauren enquired.

'No, he's doing marine biology. They're both going into their third year,' Mrs Dodd said, her eyes clouded with memories. 'I mean... were...' Her voice trailed off.

'Did they have a year out before going to university?' Matt asked, assuming they did because of their age, but wanted to double-check in case it turned out to be relevant.

'Yes, they had a gap year and travelled overseas to Australia and New Zealand,' Mr Dodd confirmed. 'They'd planned to go back sometime because they loved it so much.'

'Going back to the engagement, are you definitely sure that you had no idea it was about to happen?' Lauren asked, in case they'd now remembered something.

Mrs Dodd shook her head, her hands trembling slightly as she clasped them together. 'Maybe Finley surprised her. If she'd known, I'm sure she would have told me, even if it was meant to be a secret. We're very close.' She paused, swallowing hard. 'But, like we told you, we expected it to happen sometime, didn't we, Adrian,' she continued, turning to her husband with a haunted look in her eyes.

'Yes,' Mr Dodd replied, his voice flat.

'Were you happy about that?' Matt asked.

'Yes. Finley was a nice boy. We've always been a bit worried because his family is different from us... But... these days it doesn't matter so much, does it?' Mrs Dodd said, sounding unsure.

'What do you mean by different?' Lauren asked.

'Well, you know... they're rich and we're not... But it's not like they're snobby or anything. They always speak to us when they see us, don't they, Adrian?' Mrs Dodd looked at her husband, but he didn't seem to register her question.

'Where do they live while at university?' Lauren asked.

'In a flat with other students,' Mrs Dodd replied, her voice regaining some steadiness as she focused on the practical details.

'So they actually live together?' Matt confirmed.

'Yes, but during the holidays Jasmine lives here and Finley goes home,' Mrs Dodd said, absentmindedly smoothing the fabric of her skirt, as if trying to iron out the wrinkles in her composure.

'How was their relationship?' Lauren asked, leaning in slightly.

'It was good, of course. Jasmine was very happy. They wouldn't have got engaged if it wasn't... except...' Mrs Dodd began, stopping herself abruptly.

'What is it, Mrs Dodd?' Lauren prompted.

'I don't think this has anything to do with it, but Finley liked to gamble. A lot. I spoke to Jasmine about it the other day, and she told me it was now under control and I shouldn't worry because she's totally fine with it.'

'How did you learn about Finley's gambling problem?' Lauren asked, giving a quick glance in Matt's direction.

Was this a red flag? Especially if it had got out of hand.

'I found Jasmine crying in her room a while ago, and she confided in me,' Mrs Dodd said, her voice breaking. 'She said she couldn't stop him, and it seemed to be getting worse.'

'When was this exactly?' Lauren pushed.

'During the Easter holidays... so about five months ago,' Mrs Dodd replied, dabbing at her eyes with a tissue.

'And you didn't mention it again until the other day?' Lauren asked, looking from one parent to the other.

'We spoke several times about it. At the start of the summer holidays in June she was still concerned, but then the other day she said that it was all fine,' Mrs Dodd replied, her voice trembling.

Could Finley's gambling have spiralled out of control, leading to him being so desperate that he wanted to end his life? But then why would Jasmine have agreed to it?

But... What if it was a murder-suicide? It could have been. And if it was, would Henry be able to find out? He'd discuss it with Lauren later.

'Can you think of any reason why Jasmine and Finley might have taken their own lives?' Lauren asked softly.

'No, none at all,' Mr Dodd said, shaking his head vigorously. 'It's just... are you sure? I know there's a note, but it doesn't seem... I can't believe it. She was so happy when she went out yesterday...' His voice broke. 'We had a joke about... about me being obsessed with my garden. She didn't act like that was going to be the last time I'd see her...'

'We don't know for sure, Mr Dodd, but unfortunately that's what the evidence is indicating. I'm sorry to ask at this time, but we'd like to take a quick look around Jasmine's room, if we may,' Lauren asked, standing up.

Matt followed suit.

'Yes, I'll take you,' Mrs Dodd said, beginning to stand.

'No, you stay here. We'll be fine on our own,' Lauren said, holding up her hand.

'Okay. It's the second room on the right.' Mrs Dodd dropped back down on the sofa.

Matt and Lauren left the room and climbed the stairs in silence. He didn't want to speak until they were out of earshot.

'We shouldn't have mentioned Finley, ma'am,' Matt said once they'd gloved up, gone into the bedroom and closed the door behind them.

'I know, but they'd guessed. I'm sure they'll keep it to themselves,' Lauren said, with a sigh.

'It's very tidy,' Matt said, inspecting the meticulously organised room, his eyes resting on the neat row of framed photos on the wall of Jasmine with Finley and her friends.

'Yes, it is. I'll take the wardrobe and you the dressing table. It will have to be a cursory look for now because we need to get to Finley's house. We can come back if necessary.'

Matt pulled open the top drawer, his eyes skimming over the neatly arranged make-up and stationery but could see nothing that might give a clue as to what had happened.

'Nothing here, ma'am.'

'Nor here,' Lauren replied.

They left the room and went downstairs, where Mr and Mrs Dodd hadn't moved.

'Did you find anything?' Mr Dodd asked.

'We only took a quick look but nothing stood out,' Lauren answered. 'Before we leave, please could you give us the names of Jasmine's friends? We'd like to speak to them.'

'We don't know all of her friends from university,' Mrs Dodd said. 'But her best friend from school, who's also at Southampton University, is Ruby Bennington. They're inseparable. She knows everything about Jasmine.'

'Thank you,' Lauren said. 'I'm going to arrange for a family liaison officer to be with you throughout the investigation. They'll be able to answer any questions you might have related to what's going on with the postmortem and anything else we're looking into. But here's my card if you'd rather speak to me. You can call me anytime.' Lauren handed her card to Mrs Dodd, who took it from her and placed it on the coffee table without even looking at it.

'Can we see our girl?' Mr Dodd asked, looking at his wife, rather than at Lauren. His shoulders were hunched, and his hands clenched tight.

'We will need a formal identification of Jasmine, which the liaison officer will arrange with you,' Lauren said.

'What about the funeral?' Mr Dodd added.

Mrs Dodd gasped, her hand flying to her mouth as tears spilt onto her cheeks. The word 'funeral' seemed to shatter what little composure she had left.

'Not yet,' Lauren explained gently. 'The pathologist is currently carrying out his investigation to confirm the cause of death. That gets reported to the coroner, who will then decide when Jasmine can be released back to you.'

'You mean confirm it was suicide?' Mr Dodd clarified, his voice filled with despair.

'Yes, that's right.'

'And if they say it wasn't?' Mr Dodd asked.

'It's best if we wait to see, rather than making guesses,' Lauren said. She stood up. 'Again, we're very sorry for your loss. We'll see ourselves out.'

As they walked to the door, the burden of the Dodds' grief weighed heavily on Matt. He glanced back one last time at the distraught parents, wishing there was more they could do for them.

Lauren's fingers had barely brushed the door handle when Mrs Dodd's voice sliced through the silence, raw with desperation.

'She wouldn't... My Jasmine would never take her own life.'

Matt and Lauren locked eyes, years of experience crystallising into shared suspicion. The mother's certainty hung heavy in the air between them.

They stepped into the hall, pulling the door closed with a soft click, but Mrs Dodd's words had already lodged themselves in Matt's mind.

FOUR

SUNDAY 10 SEPTEMBER

Lauren's eyes widened as they approached the Glenisters' residence in Alverton Road. The contrast between this property and the Dodds' modest home was impossible to ignore.

'Wow, this is very different from Jasmine's house,' she commented, her gaze sweeping over the impressive facade of the Regency stucco property that stood proudly, nestled between other similar homes, in the upmarket area of Penzance.

'Yes, it's certainly lovely and way beyond anything I'd ever be able to afford,' Matt agreed, admiration reflecting in his eyes.

Matt parked in the drive behind the only other car, a gleaming white Range Rover, and Lauren took a deep breath, steeling herself for the difficult conversation ahead. As they approached the front door, she took in the manicured lawn and carefully tended flower beds, a reminder of the normality that was about to be shattered.

Lauren pressed the doorbell, and its mellow chime echoed inside. She straightened her jacket and checked that her warrant card was easily accessible. After a moment, the door opened, revealing a young woman who bore a striking resemblance to Finley. Was she his sister?

'Are Mr and Mrs Glenister in, please?' Lauren asked politely.

The young woman's eyes flicked between them, a hint of apprehension crossing her features. 'Yes. Who shall I say is calling?'

'I'm Detective Inspector Pengelly, and this is Detective Sergeant Price.'

'Oh, what's it about?' she asked, her eyes widening slightly and her fingers tightening on the door handle, as if preparing herself for some bad news.

'We need to speak to Mr and Mrs Glenister,' Lauren replied, keeping her voice even, not wanting to give anything away at this stage.

'Um... oh... okay. That's my mum and dad. They're gardening so if you want to come inside, I'll get them for you.'

'Thank you,' Lauren said with a brief nod.

They stepped into the house and Lauren's senses were immediately overwhelmed by the grandeur of the entrance hall. The polished wooden floor gleamed under the soft light of an elegant chandelier. Family photos, that had been enlarged, adorned the walls, capturing happy moments that now seemed painfully poignant.

Lauren could hear the faint sounds of conversation and the occasional clink of gardening tools through the open windows, a final moment of routine for the Glenister family.

The wait seemed interminable and Lauren found herself studying a large oil painting on the wall, depicting a serene coastal scene. Was it a favourite family holiday spot? Would they ever want to visit the beach again?

Finally, footsteps approached and Lauren turned to see the young woman returning with her parents. Mrs Glenister, still wearing gardening gloves, had smudges of dirt on her cheek and Mr Glenister wore a worried frown, his eyes darting between the detectives.

'What is it?' Mrs Glenister asked, her voice constricted.

'Can we sit down and talk, please?' Lauren suggested, gesturing towards what she assumed was the living room.

Mrs Glenister's face paled. 'Why? What's happened? Is it Finley?' Her voice rose in pitch. Panic seemed to be setting in. 'I haven't seen him since yesterday. Usually he tells me if he won't be home, but he didn't. His bedroom door was open this morning and the bed not slept in. I didn't think anything of it, though, because sometimes he does forget.' She turned to her daughter, desperation in her eyes. 'You don't know where he is, do you, Faith?'

A knot formed in Lauren's stomach. She took a deep breath, preparing herself. 'Let's sit down and we can explain.'

Mr Glenister stepped forward. 'Come through to the drawing room,' he said, his voice gruff with what appeared to be suppressed emotion.

They followed him into a tastefully decorated room. Lauren's eyes swept over the plush sofas, the ornate fireplace, and the family photos on the mantelpiece. Lauren's chest constricted. In a few seconds she'd be shattering this carefully constructed world of domestic bliss.

They settled into their seats, the tension in the air almost palpable. Mrs Glenister sat upright on the sofa, while her husband sat next to her, one hand resting protectively on her shoulder. Faith huddled in an armchair, her eyes wide with uncertainty.

Lauren leant forward slightly. She took a deep breath. 'I'm very sorry to inform you, but this morning Finley's body was found on Porthcurno Beach.'

The reaction was immediate and heartbreaking. Faith let out a gasp, her hand flying to her mouth. Mrs Glenister crumpled, her body sagging as if all strength had left her, and Mr Glenister's grip on his wife's shoulder increased, his knuckles rigid.

'Did he drown?' Mr Glenister asked.

'No, he wasn't near the water. He was with Jasmine Dodd and we believe they might have taken their own lives,' Lauren said.

'No!' Mrs Glenister cried out, shaking her head vehemently. Tears streamed down her face. 'Why would Finley want to... why would Jasmine want to... kill themselves? They were so happy together. You're wrong. You've got to be.'

Lauren's heart ached for the mother. 'I'm very sorry, Mrs Glenister, but there was a note left beside them indicating that's what they'd done. It's currently being examined by forensics to confirm who wrote it.'

The woman remained motionless and she stared at Lauren and Matt with an expression of disbelief, her hands clasped in her lap.

Faith ran over to her mother, squeezed in next to her on the sofa and took hold of her hand. 'I'm here for you, Mum,' she said in a soothing tone, though shock was etched across her face.

Lauren allowed the family a moment of silence, giving them time to process the devastating news. She glanced at Matt, who nodded almost imperceptibly, encouraging her to continue.

'We do have to ask you some questions, if you're up to it,' Lauren said, trying to balance professionalism with compassion.

Mr Glenister nodded, his facial muscles tensed as he visibly struggled to maintain composure. 'Yes, okay,' he replied, his voice hoarse with emotion.

Lauren pulled out a notepad, her fingers tightening around the pen. Usually Matt handled the notes, but today she needed the distraction – something concrete to anchor her against the weight of delivering such devastating news twice in one day. It had worn down her usual professional armour. She couldn't allow herself to break, not here, not now.

'Do you have any idea why Finley and Jasmine would want to take their own lives?'

Mrs Glenister seemed to snap out of her trance at this question. 'No. Of course not,' she said, her voice cracking.

Lauren nodded sympathetically, before pressing on. 'We understand that Finley was a regular gambler. Do you think that could have had anything to do with it?'

Mr and Mrs Glenister glanced at each other nervously and then both looked at their daughter. That told Lauren all she needed to know.

Mr Glenister sighed heavily before speaking. 'Yes, we do know that he gambled,' he admitted, his shoulders sagging slightly. 'It had got out of control a while back, but he told us Jasmine helped him deal with it. She was a good support.'

Lauren jotted down this information, her mind already connecting dots and forming new questions. 'How long had he been gambling?'

'I blame myself,' Mr Glenister said, his voice riddled with guilt. 'When the children were small, we'd regularly go to the races. I'd let them choose a horse and then we'd place a bet. Finley would get so excited when he won. I think his love of gambling stemmed from there. He tried to hide it, but it wasn't hard for us to see what was happening. He'd ask for more money when he'd only just had his allowance. He regularly talked about horses, or football teams being in form. I'd never have taken them to the races if I'd known that—'

'It's not your fault, Dad,' Faith said, lifting her head, her tear-stained face reflecting grief and confusion. 'Or I would have been a gambler, too.'

Mr Glenister shrugged, as if not believing his daughter's words.

'Where we found them, there was a bottle of prosecco. It looked like they'd been celebrating because Jasmine was wearing a ring on her engagement finger, and there was a box close by. Do you know anything about that?' Lauren asked, anxious to move the questioning forward.

Mrs Glenister's hand flew to her throat. 'No, we don't,' she whispered, her voice barely audible. Then, seeming to gather herself, she added, 'But I'm not surprised. They've been together a long time.'

Exactly as Jasmine's family had reported it.

'Finley told me he was thinking of officially asking Jasmine to get engaged,' Faith said. 'They'd discussed it in the past but that's all. I didn't know he'd bought a ring.'

A wave of sympathy washed over Lauren as she observed Faith trying to come to grips with the tragedy.

'Were you and Finley close, Faith?' Lauren asked, hoping to gain more insight into the siblings' relationship.

Faith glanced at her parents and nodded. 'Sort of. We're like all brothers and sisters. Sometimes we got on well and sometimes we'd argue.'

'I understand,' Lauren said. 'How did you get on with Jasmine?'

Faith fiddled with the cuff on her sleeve. 'Okay. I liked her. We were both in the drama group. I got to know her better when she started seeing Finley. The three of us went to Australia and New Zealand for our gap year,' she added, a sad smile flickering across her face.

Lauren frowned. 'But aren't you younger than them?'

'Faith was put up a year at school because she was so far ahead. She left the same time as Finley,' Mrs Glenister explained.

'And after going overseas you came back to start university?' Matt asked.

'Finley and Jasmine did,' Faith explained, her voice growing stronger as she focused on the memories. 'I stayed an extra year in New Zealand because I loved it so much and had met someone.' She sighed. 'But it didn't last and I came back and started Southampton University a year after them.'

'The same uni as Finley and Jasmine,' Lauren noted, piecing together the timeline.

Faith nodded. 'Yes. I'm studying quantum physics. I'm about to go into my second year,' she said, managing a small smile through her tears.

'She's very clever,' her mother added, reaching over to pat Faith's hand. 'Finley was, too,' she added as if not wanting to disrespect her son's memory.

Lauren turned her attention back to the parents. 'How did Finley support himself while he was at university? We know that Jasmine worked during her holidays and also had a student loan.'

Mr Glenister straightened, a hint of defensiveness creeping into his posture. 'We provided for him. We gave him money, but he also has a small student loan.'

Lauren made a note, then looked up. 'Did he work at all?'

A rueful smile crossed Mr Glenister's face. 'Well, Finley was a bit of a fly-by-night when it came to work,' he admitted. 'He had several holiday jobs, but somehow never managed to keep them. We didn't mind because he did well at his studies.'

Lauren absorbed this information, her mind working to fit it into the larger picture. Was Finley unstable enough to want to end his life? She glanced at Matt, noticing the thoughtful furrow of his brow.

'Did you support his relationship with Jasmine?' Lauren asked, curious as to whether they thought her good enough.

'Well to be honest, initially we were sceptical,' Mr Glenister said. 'They were very young to be involved so seriously, and socially her background was different from ours. But once we got to know her, and had met her parents on several occasions, we were coming round to the relationship. She seemed to be a settling influence on Finley, which was a good thing.'

'Is there anything else you can tell us about Finley's recent behaviour? Anything unusual?' Lauren asked, hoping to uncover some clue that might shed light on the tragedy.

'He did seem a bit stressed lately,' Faith said. 'But I thought it was exams and stuff. They were waiting for their results to come through. He always worried about results, but there was no need.'

Lauren nodded, making another note. There was still so much they didn't know, but every detail could be crucial in understanding what had led to this tragic event.

'What about Finley's friends?' she asked, her gaze moving between the family members. 'Is there anyone in particular we should speak to?'

Mr Glenister looked at Faith.

'I suppose there's Dylan,' Faith said. 'He's Fin's closest friend. He went to our school and now shares a flat with Finley, Jasmine and some others at university.'

'What's Dylan's surname?' Lauren asked, her pen poised.

'Fairclough,' Faith replied.

'We'd like to speak to him, if you could let us have his contact details,' she said.

'I've got them,' Faith said, pulling out her phone and calling them out for Lauren.

'We'd like to take a quick look at Finley's bedroom, if we may,' Lauren said.

Mrs Glenister nodded, her movements slow and weary. 'His room's upstairs, first on the right,' she said with a shuddering sigh. 'I stripped the bed this morning and the bed linen's on the floor, so you'll have to...' She trailed off, pressing a fist to her mouth to stifle a sob.

'We won't be long and we'll be mindful of the sheets,' Lauren said, rising to her feet and gesturing for Matt to follow.

Lauren and Matt made their way to Finley's room and stood for a moment in the doorway. Several action novels were stacked on a chair, and there were posters of obscure indie bands she hadn't heard of on the wall. Clothes were draped over the chair by his desk. He certainly wasn't as neat and tidy as Jasmine. It suddenly stuck her how tragic it was for his life to have been cut short.

They pulled on gloves and Matt went over to the wardrobe while Lauren headed to the drawers. She opened each one, taking a cursory look inside. Nothing stood out as being out of the ordinary and she motioned to Matt for them to go back downstairs to the family.

'Did you find anything useful?' Mr Glenister asked when they entered the lounge and sat back down.

'No but it was helpful to see Finley's room so we can get more of an idea of what he was like,' Lauren responded. 'There were some novels on his chair. Did he read a lot?'

'Yes, he's always enjoyed reading. Not like most boys of his age...' Mrs Glenister's words seemed to catch in her throat.

'What's going to happen now?' Mr Glenister asked.

Lauren turned to him. 'The pathologist will perform a post-mortem. Once that's over and we have the results, we'll let you know. In the meantime, a family liaison officer will be with you here and keep you updated.'

Mr Glenister's face hardened, a flash of defiance in his eyes. 'We don't need one of those,' he protested gruffly.

'It's procedure. We do that any time someone has died in mysterious circumstances,' Lauren explained in a gentle but firm way, all the time maintaining eye contact.

'But it's not mysterious. You said they took their own lives,' Mr Glenister exclaimed.

Damn. She shouldn't have used the word mysterious. The pain behind his anger, and the desperate need to make sense of the senseless, was written across his face.

'Sorry, I should have said that it's not what we would call a natural death,' Lauren explained, maintaining her calm in the face of his distress. 'We're very sorry for your loss, and as soon as the postmortem is over, we'll let you know.'

'What about identifying the body?' Mrs Glenister asked, her voice shaky. 'I know that's what happens. I've seen it on TV.'

'Yes, we will require someone to identify Finley,' she replied. 'But that doesn't have to be done today. It can be done tomorrow, if you'd rather. In the meantime, if you do think of anything, please let the family liaison officer know, or you can get in touch with me directly.'

Mrs Glenister nodded, but then her composure crumbled. She started sobbing, her body shaking with the force of her grief. Mr Glenister immediately moved in to envelop his wife in a protective embrace.

Lauren stood slowly, signalling to Matt that it was time to leave. 'We'll see ourselves out,' she said softly.

Once in the car, Lauren let out a long, ragged breath. 'We need to get to the bottom of this.' Her voice was low but intense. 'The families deserves answers.'

Matt straightened in his seat, starting the engine. 'Agreed. Where do we start?'

Lauren's mind raced through the possibilities. 'We'll track down Dylan Fairclough and Ruby Bennington, and dig deeper into Finley's gambling. My gut's telling me that could be the key.'

FIVE
SUNDAY 10 SEPTEMBER

Lauren dropped off her jacket and bag and then stepped into the main area ready to brief the team. She took a long settling breath because she was still reeling from the morning's events. The image of the young couple's bodies on the beach was etched into her memory, along with the distraught faces of both families. Thank goodness every day wasn't like this one or she'd never be able to cope.

She hurried over to the large whiteboard against the far wall. The fluorescent lights buzzed overhead, casting a harsh glow on the worn carpet and cluttered desks, and the usual hum of activity seemed muted. Her team members were speaking in hushed tones, their faces drawn and serious while waiting for her to provide direction in the face of this tragedy.

Lauren glanced across at Billy, noting that the young officer, who was usually full of energy and optimism, whatever cases they were faced with, was sitting slumped at his desk, his usual spark noticeably absent. His fingers idly traced patterns on his desktop and his eyes appeared unfocused and distant. Was there something wrong?

She took a detour over to Matt, who was hanging his jacket on the coat stand at the far side of the office.

'What's wrong with Billy?' Lauren asked in a low voice, her eyes flicking towards the officer.

'He's been like this for a while,' Matt replied, tilting his head to one side and giving a small shrug. 'Because Ellie's leaving date's getting closer.'

Lauren had initially been sceptical when the two officers got together, and had debated putting an end to it, but because Ellie was only there a short time, she'd decided to let it run its course. But surprisingly it hadn't affected Billy or Ellie's work. Now that Ellie was returning to Lenchester, Lauren realised that they were going to miss her, even though Tamsin was due back at the start of next week following her accident.

'Ah, I see,' Lauren murmured, nodding thoughtfully.

'I think we should make sure to give Billy tasks that will tax him and keep him fully occupied, to keep his mind off things.'

Matt was right. The best thing for Billy right now was to focus on the job at hand, to immerse himself in the work so that his life had purpose and direction. It had always worked for her in the past. Not that she wanted to dwell too much on her life before the police.

'I agree,' she said with a determined nod, after which she turned and walked towards the whiteboard, with Matt following close behind.

'Please, can I have everyone's attention?' she called out, her voice cutting through the low murmur of conversation. All eyes turned to Lauren, and the familiar surge of anticipation washed over her. She thrived in the midst of a challenging case while guiding her team towards the truth. 'I don't know what you know so far,' she began, her gaze sweeping the room, taking in the attentive faces of her officers. 'But this morning, I came across the bodies of a young couple. Initial conclusions are that they died by suicide.'

Lauren picked up one of the marker pens and wrote the names of the victims on the board next to each other.

Shock and concern were etched on the team's faces, mirroring her own conflicted emotions.

'What do you mean, "initial conclusions", ma'am?' DC Clem Roscoe asked, his voice tense. 'Is it unclear?'

Lauren took a moment to gather her thoughts, her hands clasped in front of her. 'Well, until we hear back from the pathologist, we can't assume anything. However, having said that, there was a note with "SORRY" written on it placed beside them.'

'Is that it?' DC Jenna Moyle asked. 'That's hardly a note. It's not telling anyone anything. It sounds a bit fishy if you ask me.'

'I agree, Jenna,' Lauren said, with a sharp nod. 'It also appeared that the couple had got engaged while on the beach.'

'So that would mean they had a suicide pact after they got engaged. That's crazy,' Clem said, his brow furrowed.

'It's possible, but we can't jump to any conclusions. But having spoken to both sets of parents, we know that in the past Finley Glenister had a gambling problem. We're unsure yet whether he was still gambling.'

At this, Billy's head snapped up, the misery on his face momentarily replaced by curiosity. A glimmer of hope sparked in Lauren at seeing some of his usual enthusiasm return. 'Do you think it could be a murder-suicide?' he asked, his voice hopeful, as if desperate for any lead that might distract him from his personal woes.

Lauren turned to face Billy directly. 'Well, again, we won't know until we hear back from the pathologist. Henry suspected they might have taken some drugs. But that's all we know. We have their best friends' names. I'd like someone to contact them and ask them in for an interview.'

'Leave that to me, ma'am,' Jenna offered.

'Thanks, I'll forward their details. Someone needs to dig into Finley Glenister's gambling habit, and also let's check how prolific the pair of them were on social media, because that should give us a clue as to their states of mind.' With a decisive step, Lauren turned to the whiteboard, the squeak of the marker filling the suddenly quiet room as she wrote the names of the victims' loved ones. 'Jasmine Dodd's an only child,' she explained, her voice steady. 'Finley Glenister has a younger sister. I've arranged for FLOs to go to both households. Any questions?'

'Shall I check the CCTV?' Clem asked.

'Yes, please. We'll all get together later once we know more about the pair.'

As the team began their various tasks, Lauren couldn't shake the feeling that there was more to this case than met the eye. The note, the engagement and the gambling issues all pointed to a complex web of secrets and lies that they'd need to untangle if they hoped to bring closure to the grieving families.

She watched as her officers moved with purpose, each of them diving into their assigned tasks. She was lucky to have such an efficient team and the fact they gelled so well was in no small part thanks to Matt. When her sergeant had joined them there had been a distinct divide between her and the officers who reported to her. But Matt, with his quiet, unassuming manner, had persuaded Lauren to work *with* them, rather than simply ordering them what to do, and to trust in their abilities to get the job done in a satisfactory manner.

Jenna was already on the phone, her voice low and professional as she began contacting the victims' friends. Clem had his head bent over his computer, fingers flying across the keyboard as he looked at CCTV footage. Even Billy seemed to have found some focus, his earlier despondency replaced by a look of concentration as he pored over a social media site. And Ellie also had her head down peering at her screen.

But even as Lauren's mind raced with the details of the case, she found her thoughts drifting back to Billy and how he was going to be when Ellie left. Yes, they needed to be patient with him, but she wasn't prepared to have her team disrupted by his behaviour. She'd allow him a few days to settle back into a routine without Ellie but after that she'd make sure he toed the line.

With a heavy sigh, Lauren made her way back to her office, her steps measured and purposeful. The hustle and bustle of the main office faded as she closed the door behind her, the sudden quiet both a relief and a reminder of the extent of her responsibilities. The phone on her desk began to ring and she hurried over to answer.

'Pengelly.'

'Good morning, Lauren.' She immediately recognised the voice of her boss, DCI Mistry.

'Good morning, sir.'

'I understand we have two bodies.'

'Yes, sir. I was the person to find them. It appears they've taken their own lives but we're waiting for confirmation from the pathologist.'

'Was there anything suspicious?' Mistry asked, sounding puzzled.

'The note was very brief, and the couple seemed to be celebrating an engagement. The young man also had a gambling problem.'

'I see. Well, keep me updated on any significant developments. We won't announce the deaths to the media until cause of death has been confirmed.'

He ended the call and Lauren sat back, the weight of what lay ahead settling over her. If these deaths weren't suicide, they were dealing with something far darker. Murder committed by someone methodical enough to stage the scene. Someone who'd managed to get close enough to two young people to end their lives. And someone who might not be finished.

SIX

MONDAY 11 SEPTEMBER

The early morning air nipped at Matt's face as he and Lauren approached the hospital entrance. He'd been uneasy from the moment Lauren had called him into her office to say that Henry had asked them to visit the morgue. Lauren had offered for him to stay in the car, but he refused. It would be a downward spiral if he allowed his phobia to get the better of him. And it wasn't like they were going to be faced with some gory, headless corpse... He grimaced, hoping he hadn't jinxed it.

'Are you okay?' Lauren asked as she pushed through the hospital doors.

'Yes, why?'

'You're pulling a very strange face.'

'You know what I'm like. I was imagining what we might be faced with in the morgue. You know: a dismembered body or something.' A nervous chuckle escaped his lips. 'Are you sure Henry didn't give you any hint as to what he's got to tell us about the deaths?'

'I've already explained that all he said to me was that he wants us there straight away,' Lauren replied.

'Sorry,' he said while glancing at his watch. 'He must've been in early as it's still only eight-thirty.'

The image of Henry begrudgingly arriving at work before consuming his beloved full English cooked breakfast flashed through Matt's mind. Whatever had brought Henry in this early must be significant, and that thought did nothing to ease the knot that had formed in the pit of Matt's stomach.

'They're still short staffed; I expect his work is piling up,' Lauren said, her voice tinged with resignation. 'Like lots of places these days.'

Matt nodded, all too familiar with the strain budget cuts were putting on every department. It was common practice for anyone in their occupation to pull long hours. Still, that didn't account for why Henry had demanded they come to see him immediately.

'I'm surprised you didn't ask for more details?' he said, unable to contain his curiosity. He immediately regretted his words as he saw a flash of irritation cross Lauren's face.

'Well, I didn't. Does it really matter as we're almost there? All he said was for us to get there straight away, and I didn't bother to ask. I was in the middle of other things.' She let out another sigh, her frustration almost palpable.

Matt's concern deepened. Something was bothering Lauren beyond the early morning summons from Henry. It wasn't like her to be this on edge. What was going on with his usually unflappable boss?

'I was only asking, ma'am. I didn't mean anything by it,' he said, hoping to ease the tension. 'Is there something else going on?'

Lauren's expression softened slightly. She glanced in his direction, her eyes meeting his briefly. 'Sorry, I didn't mean to sound all snappy. It's just... You're right, there is something on my mind. Do you remember my aunt Julia?'

He did. After Lauren's parents had died, she'd lived with

her mum's sister, her husband and their two sons. To say the family skirted on the wrong side of the law was an understatement. Apart from her aunt, who wasn't like the rest of the family, Lauren had nothing to do with them now. Although recently Matt had helped Lauren deal with a dire situation that her cousins had got into.

'Yes, of course,' he said. 'Don't tell me your cousins are in trouble again.'

'I don't know. My aunt messaged me asking if we could meet.'

'Maybe she wants to reestablish contact with you.'

'Maybe. But why now? I can't be drawn into that life again.'

'Did you agree to see her?'

'I replied saying it's not a good time, but I'll be in touch soon.' Lauren sighed. 'Anyway, enough about me. Let's go inside.'

Matt pushed open the double doors to the mortuary part of the hospital, a sense of foreboding washing over him. The cold air hit him like a wall, raising goosebumps on his arms. The familiar, clinical smell of the morgue filled his nostrils, a scent he'd never quite become used to despite years on the job. Henry stood in the middle of the room, his usual dedicated focus directed at the two bodies on the stainless-steel tables. He looked up as they entered, his face stern. Matt's stomach tightened with anticipation.

'Ah, good. You're here. Finally,' Henry said, his tone carrying an urgency that made Matt's pulse quicken and his mind race with possibilities.

'We came as soon as you asked, Henry,' Lauren said, her earlier frustration replaced by professional focus.

'Sorry. I'll get straight to the point,' Henry stated, his eyes dark with concern. 'My investigation has led me to conclude we're dealing with murder.'

Matt's jaw dropped. 'So you were right that drugs were

involved. Are we now looking at a murder-suicide and if so, which of the victims is which...' His voice trailed off, his mouth suddenly dry, the implications of Henry's words beginning to sink in.

'No, this is a double murder,' Henry confirmed, his voice steady but filled with a sense of foreboding.

Matt exchanged a stunned glance with Lauren, seeing his own shock mirrored in her wide eyes. A double murder? How could that be? His mind raced to readjust all their previous assumptions about the case.

'How? What happened?' Lauren asked.

Henry cleared his throat, the sound unnaturally loud in the silent morgue. 'Forensics confirmed the presence of drugs. But the amount in their blood wasn't sufficient to kill either of them. It was enough to make them fall asleep. Come over here and I'll show you what I've concluded happened.'

They stepped forward, and Matt held his breath, steeling himself for what he was about to see. The pale bodies, with the cuts from the postmortem, were bad enough, but luckily everything else seemed intact. He forced himself to look, knowing that as a detective, he needed to face these difficult realities head-on.

'What are we looking at?' Lauren asked, leaning in closer, her eyes scrutinising the bodies intently. Matt followed her gaze.

'Can you see that light bruising around the edge of the mouth? It's only slight, not a significant amount because there wasn't a huge amount of pressure.' Henry's gloved finger hovered over the faint marks on Jasmine's mouth.

'Were they suffocated?' Matt asked, leaning in and squinting to see the subtle discolouration.

'Yes, that's my theory. These marks are on both bodies.' Henry turned to Finley and pointed to his mouth, where the marks were also evident. 'I believe their drinks were drugged with enough zopiclone to make them fall asleep. After which time they were suffocated with a cushion or pillow,' Henry concluded.

A chill ran down Matt's spine. This changed everything.

'So, we now have a full-on murder investigation. Is there anything else you can tell us, Henry?' Lauren asked.

'Yes. The alcohol level in the blood of both victims wasn't high enough to indicate that a whole bottle had been consumed. At the scene the bottle was empty and according to forensics there was no alcohol on the rug they were sitting on.'

'Could it have been tipped away in the sand?' Matt asked.

'There didn't appear to be any close by and the tide hadn't come in when the bodies were found. It might have been tipped further away, out of forensics coverage, and then the bottle replaced.'

'Or there was someone with them, who drank the rest,' Lauren suggested.

'The murderer,' Matt added. 'It would have made it much easier to drug them if the killer was on the spot.'

'How much did the victims consume?' Lauren asked.

'I'd say one to two glasses each.'

'If someone else was with them there would have been an additional glass,' Lauren said thoughtfully. 'But where is it? Henry, can you ascertain whether the drug was administered via the bottle or the individual glasses?'

'There was no residue in either of the glasses so I suspect it was the bottle, but I can't be one hundred percent certain.'

'I see. Did you discover anything else?'

'There were fibres around the mouths of both victims which have been sent for analysis,' Henry replied.

'Did these fibres came from the cushion used to suffocate them?' Matt asked.

'Yes, I believe so. It wouldn't have taken much pressure to end their lives. If they'd been suffocated by hand there'd be more marks visible on their faces, fingerprints,' Henry responded.

'What about time of death?' Lauren asked.

'Between nine-thirty and eleven-thirty on Saturday night.'

'Okay, thanks, Henry. What a good way to start the day. We've now gone from suicides to murders,' Lauren said, with a sigh.

'Did you find anything in their personal possessions?' Matt asked, wanting to ensure they had all the information they needed before leaving.

'They both had mobile phones. They're in separate evidence bags over there.' Henry nodded towards the side where the two phones were placed. 'I found them in the pockets of their clothing. Oh, and there was also something else you might find interesting.'

'What is it?' Lauren prompted.

Henry walked over to the side and picked up a small evidence bag. 'I found this in Jasmine's pocket. It's a key with an unusual design.'

Matt leant in to examine it. 'It doesn't look like a house key.'

'No, it doesn't,' Henry agreed. 'I've sent photos to the lab and they're going to run it through their database to see if we can identify where it's from.'

'Thanks, Henry. It might be nothing, but also it could be linked to the murders. Please will you let us know as soon as you hear back about the fibres?' Lauren said, heading over to where the phones were situated and picking them up.

'Will do,' Henry said, turning away from them and focusing on the bodies in front of him.

Matt and Lauren left the morgue, walking in silence.

'A double murder,' Matt mused once they were outside in the morning sun. 'I didn't see that one coming.'

'Me neither. But now I can't help wondering, with two victims killed in an identical way, what if they're not the last? What if this is just the beginning?'

SEVEN

MONDAY 11 SEPTEMBER

Lauren pushed open the door to the office, the familiar creak barely registering as she dwelled on the implications of Henry's revelations. She kept her hand on it until Matt, who was close behind her, was also through. The office noise dulled as they entered, the team's eyes immediately on them.

Lauren squared her shoulders, drawing herself up to her full height. The news she was about to deliver would change everything, and she needed their full focus. 'Okay, everyone, listen up,' she announced, pausing while she made eye contact with each team member. 'We have been with the pathologist, who reported that Jasmine Dodd and Finley Glenister didn't take their own lives. We're now looking at murder.'

Lauren listened to the collective intake of breath as her words sank in and she watched her team's expressions shift from surprise to concern, to determination. Whoever said that working in Cornwall was a soft option, knew nothing. It was as intense as plenty of other, much larger, forces in the country.

'Murder? Not murder-suicide, then?' Clem asked, his eyebrows shooting up in surprise, the pen he was holding dangling forgotten in the air.

She nodded to Matt, encouraging him to elaborate, considering that had been his initial thought. 'That's exactly what I asked, Clem, because I couldn't see it being anything else, under the circumstances. But it turns out that both victims were drugged, although not given enough to kill them, and once they were asleep, or certainly incapacitated, they were suffocated with a cushion or pillow that was placed over their faces.' Matt's face was grave as he relayed the chilling details. 'It's also possible that the murderer was celebrating with the couple for at least some of the time—'

'How do you know?' Clem interrupted.

'Because there's some missing prosecco, which wasn't in the victims' systems, and the bottle was empty. Forensics checked and didn't find any spilt on the blanket or on the sand,' Matt explained.

'But we don't know for definite,' Clem added, probing further.

'No, but it makes sense, especially as there's no sign of struggle. The murderer could have had a glass of prosecco and, at some point, slipped some of the zopiclone into the bottle.'

'Or their glasses,' Billy suggested.

'Henry believes it's most likely that the bottle had the drugs in it.'

'Isn't zopiclone a prescription sleeping pill?' Jenna asked.

'Yes, that's right, which means it could have been readily available to the murderer. It's the most common one prescribed, I believe,' Matt replied.

'Assuming they wouldn't have given a stranger a celebratory drink, they must have known their killer,' Jenna added.

'It seems likely, but we're not ruling out anything,' Lauren said.

'Yes, because there could have been another person on the beach who saw them celebrating and came over to offer their congratulations,' Billy said.

'But that would mean someone was on the beach, with the drugs and intending to murder the couple,' Clem said, shaking his head. 'And carrying a cushion to finish them off. I don't buy it.'

'Well, when you put it that way,' Billy conceded.

'We have to be open to all possibilities. It's too early to make any suppositions,' Lauren said, punctuating each word with a tap of her finger on the desk. 'In the meantime, I have the victims' mobile phones.' Lauren held up the evidence bags she had in her hand. The plastic crinkled in her grip, a tangible reminder of the lives lost. 'Ellie, see if you can access them. At least that way we can check what's there straight away and see if there's anything that will help with the investigation. There might be texts regarding meeting someone on the beach.' Lauren handed the phones to the officer. Her gaze was steady, conveying the urgency of the task.

Ellie was their best bet for getting into the phones quickly.

'Yes, ma'am,' Ellie said, taking the phones and immediately setting to work, her fingers moving swiftly over one of the devices.

Lauren turned to the other officers, already mapping out the next steps of the investigation. 'Billy, I want you to recheck the victims' social media accounts but this time be cognisant of the fact they were murdered. There might be something on there that points to them being targeted which you'd missed before. A negative, or sarcastic comment, maybe.'

'Yes, ma'am.'

'You know, this could all be related to Finley's gambling,' Jenna interjected, her voice thoughtful.

Lauren nodded. 'Yes, that's something we need to investigate. And we also need to revisit both sets of parents to inform them of what we now know. It's even more imperative for us to speak to Jasmine and Finley's friends. Did you arrange that,

Jenna?' she asked, turning to the officer, her eyebrow raised in question.

'I had no joy yesterday but I'm planning to try again short-ly,' Jenna said, her tone slightly defensive, a hint of frustration flashing in her eyes.

'Okay, well do it now, please. And then start looking into Finley's gambling. It was mentioned by both victims' families.'

'Yes, ma'am,' Jenna said.

'Also, we need to know more about the engagement ring. According to the box it came from Joseph Jones, a small inde-pendent jewellery shop in the centre of Penzance. I know where it is but haven't visited. Matt, after we've been to the victims' homes, we'll stop off there.'

'Yes, ma'am,' Matt replied.

Lauren swept her gaze across the room, taking in each offi-cer's determined expression. 'CCTV needs to be re-checked as well. We're looking for cars arriving and leaving the area around Porthcurno Beach on Saturday between the hours of nine-thirty and eleven-thirty. It's a pain because there are no cameras close to the beach but you might see something that will assist us.'

'I checked yesterday and saw nothing unusual, but will look again, ma'am,' Clem said.

'Thanks. Also, people living close to the beach should be questioned. Clem, please contact uniform and ask them to send out some officers. Remember, we don't want to inform the public that we're dealing with two murders yet.'

'Leave that with me, ma'am.'

'Okay, is everyone clear on what they're doing?' she asked, her voice firm yet encouraging. She needed them all at their best for this investigation.

Before anyone could answer, Matt's phone pinged. He pulled it out of his pocket.

'I'm sorry, ma'am. I've had a text from my mum, asking me

to phone straight away. She wouldn't do that while I'm at work unless there was something wrong.'

Lauren frowned, hoping that it was nothing serious. 'Okay, no problem, Matt. You make the call, and find me when you're ready to go. I'll be in my office.'

She turned back to the team. 'Everybody clear on what they're doing?' she repeated.

The team nodded, their faces reflecting the gravity of the situation.

'Remember, our job isn't just to find out who's behind these deaths, but also the motive. Why were these two young people murdered? This wasn't random because of the use of drugs. Until we discover the motive, we won't know if anyone else's life is at risk.'

She mentally went through the possibilities. Was it connected to Finley's gambling? A jealous ex-partner? Or something darker and more complex that they hadn't yet considered?

With a final nod to the team, Lauren turned and headed into her office. She closed the door behind her and took a moment to collect herself. Then she moved to her desk, and began updating the case file, while deliberating on the complex web of information they needed to untangle.

She couldn't believe they were faced with yet another murder investigation. The coming days would be challenging, filled with long hours and potentially frustrating dead ends. She'd have to update the DCI and discuss whether he wanted to hold a press conference yet.

* * *

Matt left the office in a hurry. Was it Dani? Was she sick, or something worse?

Once alone in the corridor, he called his mum, each unanswered ring amplifying his anxiety.

Why wasn't she answering?

He began pacing – his footsteps echoing loudly in the empty hallway – while at the same time he ran his free hand through his hair.

Finally, as he was about to hang up, the phone was answered.

'Hello.' His mum sounded breathless and strained, immediately alerting him.

'Mum, it's me.' He tried to keep his voice steady, overcoming the unease gripping him.

'Oh, Matt, I'm sorry to bother you at work, but your dad's been taken to hospital,' she replied, her voice thick with worry.

It was like the floor had dropped out from under him as dozens of terrible scenarios bombarded him. His grip on the phone tightened.

'What? Why? What's wrong?' he asked urgently, his pitch rising with every question. He could hear the panic in his own voice but was powerless to control it.

'Well, he was walking into the kitchen earlier, and it looked like he stumbled and grabbed onto the table to steady himself. I said, "Are you okay, love?" but when he looked at me, his eyes seemed all glazed and confused. I rushed over and grabbed his arms, helping him sit down in one of the chairs. But he was so disoriented, Matt. It's like he wasn't fully there with me,' his mum explained, her words spilling out in a rush. 'I called for an ambulance and they said it sounded like he might have had a stroke. The paramedics agreed and they've taken him to the hospital.'

Matt's breath caught in his throat. This couldn't be happening. Not to Dad. He'd always been so strong and healthy. He leant against the wall for support as his legs threatened to give way.

'How was he when they took him to the hospital? Did he

recognise you?' Matt asked, desperately seeking any positive sign to cling to.

'Yes, he seemed to. He was talking when the paramedics got here but not making much sense. They told him to try to lift his arms and he thought he did but it was only his right arm that moved. His left stayed still.'

'Okay, left-sided symptoms, that does sound like a potential stroke,' Matt said, trying to dredge up anything he remembered from the basic first aid courses he'd taken. 'But if he's talking, that's a good sign. Maybe it was a minor one, a TIA or something. I can't remember exactly what that stands for.'

'The paramedic did say something about a TIA, I remember now,' his mum confirmed.

'Why didn't you go with Dad in the ambulance?' Surely she'd have wanted to be with him.

'Dani needs collecting from nursery later and I wasn't sure if you'd be around to help, so I stayed here.'

'Don't you worry about Dani, Mum. I'll collect her. Where have they taken Dad?'

'Truro hospital.'

'I'll be home shortly and will take you over there. I don't want you driving yourself.'

The thought of his mother behind the wheel in her current state sent a fresh wave of anxiety through him.

There was a heavy pause before his mum replied. 'Okay, if you're sure. What about work?'

'Lauren won't mind. Did the paramedics say anything else before they left?'

'Not really. Your father was grumbling that I shouldn't have called them and he was fine. Being his usual stubborn self. But I've never seen him like that before, Matt. So confused and weak. I'm scared,' she said, her voice breaking.

He swallowed hard. 'I know, Mum. I'm scared too. But

Dad's a fighter. He'll get through this. And we'll be right there with him every step of the way. I'll be home in ten minutes so sit tight and we'll head to hospital together. You can stay with him while I sort out Dani.'

After a few more words of encouragement, Matt ended the call. How would his mum cope if anything happened to his dad? The thought was almost too terrible to contemplate.

He hurried towards the outside door to Lauren's office, deliberately avoiding going through the main room. He didn't trust himself to hold it together in front of the team. He gave a knock and opened the door.

Lauren glanced up from her computer, her welcoming smile immediately morphing into a look of concern when she saw him.

'I'm sorry, ma'am. I have to leave right now. It's my dad. He's been rushed to the hospital. They think he's had a stroke.' The words tasted bitter on his tongue. Saying it out loud made it feel entirely too real, and he had to fight back a sudden wave of nausea.

Lauren raised a hand to her mouth, her eyes widening. 'Oh Matt, I'm so sorry. Of course you must go. Don't give work another thought. We'll manage here.'

'I have to pick up Dani from nursery later. I don't know when I'll be back,' he continued, feeling guilty for abandoning the case but knowing he had no choice. His daughter's face flashed in front of his eyes. How on earth was he going to explain this to her. She'd already lost her mum; would she think that her grandpa was going for good too, and—

'You take all the time you need.' Lauren's instant words cut into his thoughts. 'We've got things covered. Concentrate on your family. They need you. Keep me updated on your dad's condition.' She gestured with her hand for him to leave.

'I will. Thanks,' Matt replied gratefully, his throat

constricting with emotion at her kindness and understanding. He turned to head towards the door into the main office, then hesitated, a dark thought bubbling up from the recesses of his mind. 'What if... what if he doesn't...' He couldn't bring himself to finish the awful thought, the words sticking in his throat like shards of glass.

'You can't think like that,' Lauren said, her eyes locking with his, radiating reassurance. 'You need to be strong. Send your mum my best wishes.'

Matt nodded wordlessly, not trusting himself to speak. He pushed open the door to the office, stopping by Ellie's desk just long enough to choke out that he had to leave because of a family emergency. He grabbed his jacket, the fabric rough against his suddenly hypersensitive skin, and practically ran from the building.

The short walk to his car felt like an eternity. Each step seemed to take monumental effort, as if he were wading through treacle. The bright sunlight outside was like a cruel joke, at odds with the darkness threatening to engulf him. He fumbled with his car keys, dropping them once, before managing to unlock the door. He was desperate to get to the hospital and see with his own eyes that his dad was still breathing, still fighting.

He slid into the driver's seat and started the engine.

'Please let him be okay,' Matt muttered to himself over and over as he sped home. The words were like a mantra, while he prayed to whatever higher power might be listening.

The streets of Penzance blurred past his window; familiar landmarks reduced to indistinct shapes as he focused solely on getting home as quickly as possible.

A lone tear streaked down his cheek and he swiped it away impatiently, angry at himself for this momentary weakness. He had to be the strong one now: for his mum and Dani. He needed to put on a brave face and hold them together.

He pulled up outside his parents' house and took a deep,

steadying breath. Glancing at his reflection in the rearview mirror, he barely recognised the pale, scared face staring back at him. With a supreme effort of will, he schooled his features into a mask of calm determination. He could do this. He had to do this. For his mum, for Dani and, most of all, for his dad.

EIGHT

MONDAY 11 SEPTEMBER

Lauren sat at her desk, her fingers absentmindedly tracing the worn edge of her notepad as Matt's news settled over her. The fear in his eyes when he'd told her about his father had struck deep – she'd never seen her usually steady sergeant so shaken. Her chest tightened at the thought of what he must be going through, especially with young Dani to consider. Matt had been her rock since joining the team, both professionally and personally, and now he needed their support.

The practical part of her mind nudged at her. They'd have to reorganise, adapt and make sure Matt had the space he needed to be with his family, while keeping the investigation on track. But those were tomorrow's problems. Right now, her thoughts were with her friend and the long night ahead of him at the hospital.

She hoped that Mr Price was going to be okay. She'd met him on several occasions and the man had always been friendly and welcoming. The same as Matt's mum. Lauren enjoyed being in their company. Matt was very lucky to have such a loving family. Very different from hers in so many ways.

Taking a deep breath, Lauren stood up, smoothed down her

trousers and then headed back into the main office. She cleared her throat to get everyone's attention, waiting until all eyes were on her before speaking.

'Okay, I'm sure you know by now that Matt's had to leave. His father's ill and has been taken to the hospital,' she announced solemnly. A murmur of concern and sympathy rippled through the room. Lauren held up a hand for quiet, her authoritative gesture silencing the chatter almost immediately. 'Matt will keep us updated on how his dad's doing, but in the meantime we have to manage without him.'

'When he calls, please tell him we're thinking of him,' Jenna said, concern etched on her face. 'I don't want to bother him by messaging because—'

'I understand,' Lauren said, interrupting. 'I'll pass on every-one's good wishes. Obviously he won't be coming with me to speak to the victims' parents, so Jenna, I'd like you to. We'll explain the pathologist's findings and get their thoughts on what might have occurred. They might be able to identify someone with a grudge against the couple.'

'Yes, ma'am,' Jenna replied. 'I've contacted Jasmine and Finley's friends. Dylan Fairclough's coming in this afternoon but Ruby Bennington's out of the country until Thursday. She's overseas with her parents on a pre-planned trip, which is frus-trating, especially now.'

Lauren frowned, as she processed this information. 'Did you explain to Ruby why we wish to interview to her?'

'I had to, unfortunately, but all I said was that Jasmine and Finley had died. I didn't give any explanation. She was obvi-ously devastated by the news, but the family's flights were already booked and it would be almost impossible for them to change their plans and return earlier.' Jenna's shoulders slumped slightly.

'Did you explain to Dylan Fairclough the reason for asking him in?' Lauren pressed, her eyes narrowing slightly as she considered the implications of being unable to speak to Ruby until later in the week.

Jenna nodded. 'Yes. I had no choice because he asked what it was about and I didn't want to lie to him. But again I didn't let him know the cause. He sounded stunned by the news.'

'You did the right thing,' Lauren assured her. 'It wasn't an easy task, but it had to be done. We'll speak with Dylan later.' She turned to address the rest of the team. 'One thing we can deduce is that Ruby Bennington couldn't have been the mystery person with Finley and Jasmine on Saturday night, since she was out of the country. That eliminates her as a potential suspect or witness, in terms of physically being present for the engagement and murders. That doesn't mean we ignore her totally. She might have been an accessory.'

'What about Dylan Fairclough as a suspect?' Clem asked, leaning forward in his chair, his eyes bright with interest. 'I assume he's a person of interest.'

'No one's excluded. I want someone to research into him.' She glanced at Billy. 'I'll leave that to you.'

'Yes, ma'am,' Billy responded with a sharp nod.

'And we'll question him in detail when he arrives,' Lauren added. She checked her watch. 'Okay, let's get moving. Jenna and I will head over Finley's parents first, then go to Jasmine's and after that the jewellery shop.' Lauren caught Jenna's eye and inclined her head towards the door. 'I'll drive.'

The drive to the Glenisters' home was quiet. Losing Matt, even temporarily, was a huge setback.

'Nice house,' Jenna muttered, as they pulled up outside.

'Yes,' Lauren agreed, as she came to a halt. She took a moment to centre herself, drawing in a deep breath before speaking. 'I'll take the lead on this, but I want you to observe their reactions closely. Look for anything that seems off or insincere. We have to consider the possibility that the killer is someone close to the victims.'

Jenna raised an eyebrow in disbelief. 'You don't seriously think they could have been involved, do you?'

'Honestly? I'm not ruling anyone out at this point,' she replied grimly, her eyes meeting Jenna's. 'But I doubt they were. The main thing is that we keep an open mind and listen to what they have to say.' With that, she climbed out of the car and marched up to the front door with Jenna trailing in her wake.

Mrs Glenister answered, her eyes red-rimmed and puffy. A pang of sympathy at the woman's grief-stricken face hit Lauren, but she kept her expression dispassionate, years of experience helping her maintain a professional composure. 'Hello, Mrs Glenister. This is DC Moyle. She's with me today. May we come in? I'm afraid we have some additional news to share with you.'

Lauren glanced over the shoulder of the woman. Where was the FLO? They should have been answering the door, and not left it to the grieving parents.

'Yes, come in,' Mrs Glenister said, her voice hoarse. She stepped back to allow them entry, her movements slow and heavy with grief.

'Hasn't the family liaison officer arrived yet?' Lauren asked, a note of concern creeping into her voice.

'No,' the woman replied, shaking her head wearily.

Lauren would look into that when they left.

They followed Mrs Glenister into the drawing room where a grey-faced Mr Glenister was slumped on the sofa, staring blankly at a framed photograph in his hands. Lauren caught sight of a smiling Finley, his arm slung around his father's shoulders. The sight sent a pang through her chest. And now her words were about to shatter their world even further.

Seating herself in a chair across from the couple, Lauren leant forward slightly, clasping her hands together in her lap. 'Mr and Mrs Glenister, I want to start by offering you once again our deepest condolences for your loss.'

Mr Glenister raised his eyes to meet hers, his gaze haunted. 'Thank you,' he replied roughly, his voice thick with emotion. 'It still doesn't feel real. I keep expecting Finley to come bounding through the door, grinning that cheeky smile of his.' His voice broke on the last word, and Lauren had to fight the urge to reach out and comfort him.

'I wish I could tell you this will get easier soon but the truth is, losing a child is an unbearable pain that never really goes away. All you can do is take it one day, one hour, one minute at a time.' As soon as the words left Lauren's mouth, she wondered if they sounded trite. It wasn't as if Lauren had children of her own, but that didn't stop her from knowing the pain losing a child could cause. She'd witnessed other families in the same position.

Mrs Glenister dabbed at her eyes with a crumpled tissue, her hand trembling. 'What's this news you have to tell us?'

Lauren took a deep breath, steeling herself for their reaction. 'I'm sorry to tell you that the couple didn't take their own lives, as initially believed. We're treating Finley and Jasmine's deaths as suspicious.'

'You mean they were murdered?' Mr Glenister said, his voice rising in disbelief.

'Murdered?' A voice came from behind them, sharp with shock.

Lauren turned to see Finley's sister enter the room, her eyes wide with dawning horror.

'Yes, I'm sorry,' Lauren said sympathetically. 'We're doing everything we can to discover what happened. Can you think of anyone who might bear a grudge against the couple?' Lauren asked, directing her question at Faith, who had sat on the chair opposite the sofa.

'No,' Faith said, shaking her head.

'Have any of you noticed anything unusual lately? Someone hanging around outside the house perhaps? Any unfamiliar faces?' Lauren asked, looking at each one of them in turn.

The family exchanged glances, their expressions a mix of confusion and growing unease.

'No,' Mrs Glenister said, her voice hardly audible.

'Was Finley worried about anything?' Lauren asked.

'No, but he didn't really confide in us,' Mrs Glenister said with a sniff, her shoulders slumping further.

'Did he confide in you, Faith?' Lauren asked, returning her attention to the young woman.

'Sometimes. But I've been busy recently and we haven't seen much of each other,' Faith replied, her voice so quiet Lauren had to strain to hear.

'So you don't know if there was anything on his mind,' Lauren confirmed.

'No, sorry.'

Lauren turned her attention to Mr and Mrs Glenister. 'We'd like to take another look at Finley's room. Go through his belongings in more detail. Even the smallest thing could be the key to bringing Finley and Jasmine's killer to justice.'

After the Glenisters agreed, Lauren and Jenna went upstairs, gloved up, and began searching.

Jenna sifted through the contents of a desk drawer, her movements methodical and precise. 'I haven't found much yet,' she reported without glancing up. 'Receipts, concert ticket stubs, scraps of paper. Nothing that really points to trouble in Finley's life or hints at who might have wanted to hurt him.'

'Keep looking,' Lauren urged, her eyes checking the room for anything out of place. She moved to the bedside table, carefully opening the drawer and scrutinising its contents.

'Hang on a minute. There's a load of betting slips here,' Jenna said, looking up with a frown. 'These are dated from last week. If he's got the slips does that mean he's lost? Wouldn't he have to hand them in to collect any winnings?'

'I'm not sure,' Lauren said, her brow furrowed in thought as she headed over to where Jenna stood. 'Drop them into an evidence bag and we'll take them with us. There doesn't seem anything else untoward here. Nothing pointing to a reason for him being murdered.' She gave a frustrated sigh. 'We'll say our goodbyes to the family and then head to Jasmine's parents' house. On the way I need you to phone the station and find out where the FLO is. They should've been here by now.'

'Yes, ma'am,' Jenna said. 'Those poor parents. What a nightmare. I hope we can solve the case soon. To at least give them some closure.'

'Me too, Jenna. Me, too,' Lauren replied, her voice soft but filled with resolve.

Before leaving Finley's room, Lauren took one last look around, committing every detail to memory. As so often happened at the start of murder investigations, she couldn't shake the feeling that they were missing something crucial, some vital clue. But for now, all they could do was keep pushing forward, following every lead and hoping that the truth would eventually emerge.

NINE

MONDAY 11 SEPTEMBER

Lauren stepped out of the Glenisters' house, their anguished faces indelibly etched on her mind. She breathed in the crisp autumn air, trying to clear her head and refocus on the task at hand. The sun was high in the sky now, its warmth contrasting with the chill from inside.

'Right, let's head to Jasmine's parents' house,' Lauren said with a sigh, her voice betraying her weariness. It was bad enough speaking to one family and witnessing their grief, but two... that was off the scale.

'Yes, ma'am,' Jenna replied, as they climbed into the vehicle. 'Do you think Finley's gambling was a factor in their deaths?'

Lauren shook her head slowly. 'I don't know. I really don't know. I mean, why would you kill someone who owed you money? Then you'd never get it back. What do you think?' She started the car, the familiar rumble of the engine doing little to calm her.

'The same as you,' Jenna said, her voice tinged with frustration. 'We don't yet know what else has been going on in the couple's lives. Hopefully their friends will be able to give us more insight into that. Although you'd think that if anyone knew, it would be Faith, considering she was close to both of them. But she was in shock. She might come up with something once she's had time to think.'

Lauren nodded, her eyes fixed on the road ahead as she navigated through the quiet streets of Penzance. 'Also we might get something useful from Jasmine's family,' she said, trying to remain optimistic, as the gnawing sense that this case would not have a simple resolution nagged at the back of her mind.

Lauren rolled her neck slightly, trying to ease some of the tension in her taut shoulders as she drove.

'It never ceases to amaze me, ma'am, that when someone, or something, appears normal, deep down there are other things going on,' Jenna mused, as she gazed out of the front window.

Lauren nodded, her lips pressed into a thin line. 'It happens all the time in this job. We need to dig into everything that's happened between Jasmine and Finley, however small and apparently inconsequential; you never know where we might find some answers.' She came to a stop at a red light, mentally running through their next steps. 'The jewellery shop might give us something to work with.'

The light turned green and Lauren accelerated, the familiar landmarks of Penzance blurring past the windows.

'Yes. Knowing when he bought the ring might help us establish a timeline, at least.'

'One thing we do know is that the murder wasn't robbery related,' Lauren said. 'Because surely they'd have taken the ring if that was the case, and there'd have only been an empty box on the sand.'

Lauren tossed a glance in Jenna's direction and noticed the officer's eyes had widened. What had she thought?

'That's right, ma'am. And if it was to do with money Finley owed from gambling then why not take the ring as part compensation. I keep coming back to what we discussed earlier. That it's someone who knew them. Nothing else makes sense. Although the missing prosecco's a mystery. If someone else was celebrating with them, then where's the third glass?'

Lauren mentally kicked herself as she slapped her free hand lightly against her leg in frustration. 'Damn, I forgot to ask Mr and Mrs Glenister if any of their glasses had gone missing. Remind me to do that when we see Jasmine's parents, if I forget again.'

'Yes, ma'am,' Jenna said. 'I'll also contact the FLO at the Glenisters' place, once they've arrived, and ask them to find out.'

They pulled up outside the Dodd house and, once again, Lauren took a moment to compose herself before exiting the car. It was important that she put across an image of being calm and professional.

Jenna knocked on the door, and a small sense of relief surged through Lauren when the familiar face of family liaison officer Tracie appeared. The family were in excellent hands. 'Morning, ma'am.'

'I'm glad to see you're with the parents. There's no FLO at the Glenisters' house yet,' Lauren said, her brow furrowing with concern.

Tracie shook her head and tutted. 'I know, ma'am. But there's definitely one on the way. They had to be called in from another station. I'm sorry it's taking so long.'

'It's not your fault. We need more FLOs – but whether the budget will allow one...' She paused. 'That's a discussion for another time. We're here to deliver some news,' Lauren said, steeling herself for another difficult conversation. 'It's turned out that the deaths are suspicious.'

Tracie's eyes widened. 'Crikey, that's going to be a shock.'

'Are they in the lounge?'

'Yes. You go through and I'll put on the kettle. I expect they're both going to need a strong cup of sweet tea.'

When Lauren and Jenna entered the lounge, Jasmine's parents didn't appear to have moved since the previous day. They were seated on the sofa next to one another. Lauren sat on one of the easy chairs opposite them and Jenna took the other.

'Mr and Mrs Dodd, I'm sorry to disturb you again, but we do have some news,' Lauren began.

'What is it?' Mrs Dodd asked anxiously. There was fear in the woman's eyes, as if she was bracing herself for even more bad news.

Lauren met their eyes directly. 'We're now treating the deaths of Jasmine and Finley as suspicious.'

'What do you mean *suspicious*?' Mr Dodd repeated, his voice rising slightly. 'Are you saying they were killed?'

Lauren nodded solemnly. 'That's our working theory at the moment, after receiving feedback from the pathologist.'

'Oh my God...' Mrs Dodd said, her hand flying up to her mouth.

Lauren leant forward slightly. 'I know this is hard, but we wondered if we could ask you a few more questions.'

'Yes,' Mr Dodd said, his voice hoarse.

'One area we're investigating is whether someone had a grudge against either of them. Are you aware of anything?'

'No, not that we know of,' Mr Dodd replied slowly, shaking his head. His arm tightened around his wife's shoulders, a gesture of support and comfort.

'They're a couple of kids,' Mrs Dodd added, her voice so quiet Lauren had to strain to hear. 'Who would want to—' Her voice broke and tears filled her eyes.

'That's what we need to find out,' Lauren said gravely. 'Have you noticed anyone hanging around recently? Any strangers?' She searched their faces for any flicker of recognition or uncertainty.

'No, not at all,' Mrs Dodd replied, appearing perplexed.

'Do you have a set of champagne glasses, Mrs Dodd?' Lauren asked, shifting gears slightly.

'Why are you asking?' A look of confusion crossed Mrs Dodd's face, her hands twisting in her lap.

'Jasmine and Finley had been drinking from champagne glasses when they were on the beach,' Lauren explained. 'We wondered where they'd got the glasses from.'

'Oh... well yes, I do have some in the kitchen.'

'Would you mind checking to see if they're all there, please?' Lauren asked.

'Yes, of course.'

Mrs Dodd rose from her seat and hurried out of the room.

Lauren turned to Mr Dodd. 'We'd like to take another, more careful, look at Jasmine's room please.'

Mr Dodd closed his eyes for a couple of seconds, as if picturing his daughter's bedroom. 'Of course, if you think it will help.'

They sat in silence for a few seconds until Mrs Dodd returned, her footsteps quick and light on the carpeted floor. 'They're all there,' she reported, a hint of confusion in her voice.

Lauren frowned slightly. They'd check to see if the couple had used glasses from the Glenister house. Although Finley could've bought them himself.

'Thank you. We won't take up any more of your time right now. We'll just pop up to Jasmine's room.'

'Why do you need to go in there again?' Mrs Dodd asked.

'We'd like to be more thorough than yesterday,' Lauren explained.

Lauren and Jenna made their way upstairs in silence, their footsteps echoing in the quiet house.

'Goodness, she's neat,' Jenna remarked, once they were inside and they'd both glanced around at the orderly space.

Even the various photos pinned to the corkboard on the

wall were perfectly aligned, showing Jasmine's bright smile as she stood with her arm linked through her friends', or when she was with Finley.

'Yes, very,' Lauren agreed.

There was nothing out of the ordinary, just the usual clothes, make-up, a big stuffed teddy bear, and other trinkets. Nothing that seemed likely to shed light on the murders. A growing sense of frustration gnawed at Lauren.

'I can't see anything here that's going to help us,' Lauren said finally, unable to keep the disappointment from her voice. 'Henry found an odd-shaped key on her. Is there anything in here that's locked?'

'Not so far,' Jenna said. 'Oh, hang on... What's this?' Jenna stood on her tiptoes and pulled down a small raffia box with a faded honey-gold weave. It had a brass clasp. She tried the lid. 'It's locked.'

'Put it in an evidence bag and I'll ask Henry to send over the key.'

'Shall we mention it to Mr and Mrs Dodd?' Jenna asked.

'Yes. Where's her laptop? We'll take that, too.'

'It's in a case by the dressing table,' Jenna said, dropping the box into an evidence bag and then heading over to pick up the laptop.

They went downstairs and returned to the lounge. 'Mr and Mrs Dodd, we're taking Jasmine's laptop with us and also this box.' Lauren nodded to Jenna, who held out the bag containing the box.

'Please be careful with it,' Mrs Dodd said. 'It belonged to my mum and when she died, she left it to Jasmine because she'd always loved it.'

'Do you have the key for it?'

'No, Jasmine does. I mean, did. Wasn't it in the box?' Mrs Dodd asked.

'No. We did find a key with Jasmine and we're going to see

if it fits. I promise that we'll take care of the box. We'll let Tracie know if we have any updates for you.'

They headed out to the car and Lauren let out a sigh. The visit to Jasmine's room had yielded little, apart from the box – could that be the key to the two murders?

TEN

MONDAY 11 SEPTEMBER

Lauren drove back into the centre of Penzance, her mind churning with the details of the case. She parked around the corner from Union Street, and walked with Jenna the short distance to the small jewellery shop, a charming building with an old-fashioned front that seemed to belong to a different era.

Pausing for a moment, Lauren took in the display window. Delicate necklaces were draped over chrome stands and rings nestled in crushed-velvet-lined boxes, all bathed in the warm glow of carefully positioned spotlights. She opened the door and a bell pinged melodically, announcing their arrival. The interior was as inviting as the exterior and warm lighting bounced off the glass display cases. Each one was filled with a dazzling array of rings, necklaces, and earrings and under other circumstances, Lauren would have enjoyed spending time looking at all the jewellery – but not today.

Lauren glanced around the shop and observed security cameras discreetly positioned in the corners. Good. That should make their job easier, providing they'd kept the footage from when Finley had visited.

From an open door behind the counter emerged an elegant,

well-made-up woman wearing a navy dress. She looked to be in her mid-fifties and her silver hair was pulled into a neat bun. 'Good morning.' She greeted them with a warm smile, her voice soft. 'How may I help you?'

Lauren pulled out her warrant card and held it out for the woman to see. 'I'm DI Pengelly and this is DC Moyle from Penzance CID. And you are?'

'I'm Kathy Day. I own the shop.'

'We're investigating a case and are hoping you might be able to help.' Lauren pulled out her phone and, after finding the images of the ring and box, she showed it to the woman. 'Do you recognise these items?'

The woman took Lauren's phone and studied the screen closely, her brow furrowing slightly. Lauren watched her intently, years of experience allowing her to pick up on the subtle shifts in the woman's countenance. After a few seconds of concentration, recognition flickered across her face. 'Yes, of course. I sold that ring last week. Sorry, the angle of the ring in the photo made it hard for me to recognise it straight away.'

Were they about to learn something relevant to the case?

'What can you tell us about it?'

'It was a second-hand diamond and sapphire ring that we bought several months ago from a woman who no longer wanted it. The result of a failed engagement, I believe. Although please don't quote me on that. We cleaned it up before putting it on sale. It was quite exquisite. If you'll give me a moment, I'll locate details of the transaction.'

Kathy Day moved over to the computer and while she searched for the relevant information, Lauren took the opportunity to study the shop more closely. The air was heavy with the scent of polish and leather, and it mingled with the faint perfume worn by the shop owner. Behind the counter, in the far-right corner, Lauren could see a workbench with tools neatly arranged on top, ready for repairs and adjustments. Did

Kathy Day carry them out herself, or did she employ someone?

After a couple of minutes the woman turned back to them, a satisfied look on her face. 'Here it is. The ring was purchased by a Finley Glenister, and he paid in cash. Fifteen hundred pounds.'

'Cash?' Jenna interjected, her tone curious. 'Is that unusual for such a high-priced item?'

The woman considered for a moment. 'While it's not entirely unheard of, these days most people do prefer to use cards for larger purchases.'

'Would you happen to have any CCTV footage of the transaction?' Lauren asked, taking a step closer to the counter.

'I'm certain we do,' Kathy Day replied. 'Let me pull it up on the system.'

'Thank you.'

As the woman stared at the computer screen, Lauren crossed her fingers behind her back, hoping that the CCTV footage would provide them with crucial details regarding Finley's demeanour.

'Here it is,' Kathy Day said, turning the monitor so Lauren and Jenna could see and pointing her finger at one of the people on the screen. 'That's the man who purchased the ring. He was with his friend.'

Lauren and Jenna peered at the screen, studying the slightly grainy image. The two men were standing at the counter, but their body language was tense and their faces expressing what looked like anger or frustration. Lauren leant in closer, her interest piqued. This was more revealing than she'd dared hope for.

'They don't look very happy,' Lauren murmured, more to herself than anyone else. Unhappiness surrounding an engagement ring purchase could be significant.

Kathy Day nodded, a slight frown creasing her brow. 'Now

that you mention it, I do remember there seemed to be some tension between them. They were arguing about something, but I couldn't quite make out what it was about. It wasn't a full-blown row, more like a heated disagreement, but it was definitely noticeable.'

A disagreement? Could this be a motive?

'Did you hear anything? Even a snippet of their conversation could be useful.'

Kathy Day closed her eyes, as if trying to recall the incident, and Lauren held her breath, willing the woman to remember something. Kathy finally opened her eyes and looked directly at Lauren. 'Well, I do remember the other man, the one who wasn't buying the ring, saying something about how it was a bad idea. That Mr Glenister shouldn't go through with it.'

'Really?' Lauren said, her eyes wide. 'And he definitely meant the engagement?'

'That I can't be sure of. He didn't actually use those words, but I couldn't think what else it could be. I moved away from them, to give them some privacy. I didn't want them to think I was being nosy.'

'And what happened next?' Lauren asked.

'Mr Glenister seemed to brush him off, insisting that he knew what he was doing. I'm sorry, that's all I can remember. I make a point of trying not to eavesdrop on my customers' conversations, especially if, like this one, they seem fraught.'

Lauren nodded, while contemplating the implications of this new information. Was this disagreement about the proposal, as Kathy Day believed? Or could it have been in respect of the relationship as a whole? Or maybe it was to do with something else entirely? The possibilities were endless, and at the moment impossible to determine.

She turned to Jenna. 'We'll definitely need to identify and interview this other man. He could be a key witness, or even a suspect.'

'It might be his friend Dylan Fairclough,' Jenna suggested, her voice low but excited.

Lauren nodded. Fairclough, if it was indeed him, could be the break they needed.

She turned back to Kathy Day. 'How come we can't see you on the CCTV footage?'

'That's me there,' Kathy said, pointing to the edge of a figure slightly out of frame. 'You know... in spite of the disagreement, Mr Glenister did seem happy about proposing. Nervous, but happy. He mentioned he was planning to propose at their favourite beach.'

'What made you think he was nervous?' Lauren asked.

'He was hopping from foot to foot and couldn't keep still. As soon as he saw the diamond and sapphire ring, he said, "that's the one". His friend commented about the price but Mr Glenister disagreed and said it was perfect.'

Lauren nodded, hiding the twinge of sadness she felt.

'Did he ask for a discount because he was paying cash?'

'No. He was happy to pay the full fifteen hundred pounds.' The woman paused a second. 'What's happened? Why are you asking about this?'

'I'm afraid I can't discuss the details,' Lauren said, maintaining a professional, but not unkind, tone. 'Thanks for your assistance, though. You've provided us with some valuable information.'

Lauren glanced around the shop one more time, taking in the trays of sparkling engagement rings, each piece a potential symbol of love and commitment like the ring Finley Glenister had bought. How quickly joy could turn to tragedy.

'One more thing,' Lauren said, turning back to Kathy Day. 'Did you notice anything unusual about Mr Glenister or his friend? Any behaviour that struck you as odd?'

The woman pursed her lips. 'Well, now that you mention it,

Mr Glenister did keep looking over his shoulder, as if he was worried someone might see him in here.'

Was it to do with his gambling? Did he believe they were being followed?

'And his friend? How did he act?'

'He seemed agitated, too,' the woman replied. 'Kept checking his phone and pacing a bit. At one point, he stepped outside to take a call. When he returned to the shop, that's when the disagreement began.'

Lauren nodded, filing away this information. 'Has anything else sprung to mind about the argument now we've been going through it?'

The woman shook her head. 'I'm sorry, I really can't. But...' She hesitated, then continued, 'I remember thinking that there was something else going on, other than choosing a ring. In a way, they seemed scared.'

Scared. That was an interesting choice of word. 'Thank you, you've been most helpful. If you do remember anything else, no matter how small it might seem, please don't hesitate to contact us,' Lauren said, handing the shop owner her card. 'Also, please could you email me the CCTV footage.'

The woman nodded, her face etched with concern. 'I hope you get to the bottom of whatever it is you're investigating.'

'We will,' Lauren said, her voice filled with determination. 'We won't rest until we do.'

They stepped out of the shop and the bell chimed melodiously behind them. Lauren turned to Jenna. 'We need to identify that friend as soon as possible. Do we have a photo of Dylan Fairclough?'

'No, ma'am, but we'll see him soon enough. He's coming into the station to speak to us later today.'

ELEVEN

MONDAY 11 SEPTEMBER

Lauren picked up the manila folder, which contained her somewhat skimpy notes, and took a deep breath, mentally steeling herself for the task ahead. She collected Jenna and they headed to the interview room where Dylan Fairclough was waiting for them.

'Remind me what we know about this guy?' Lauren asked as they walked.

'Not a lot, ma'am. Other than he's at uni with both Finley and Jasmine and also went to school with them. He was Finley's best friend. Billy's looking into him, as you requested, but he hasn't reported back yet.' Jenna's response was crisp and professional, but Lauren could hear the underlying tension. They were all already feeling the pressure of this case.

'And he doesn't know that the deaths are suspicious, does he?'

'No, ma'am. I only informed him of the couple's deaths. He asked me what had happened, and after I said we're still investigating and wouldn't know until the pathologist had completed his investigation, he didn't pursue it.'

'Right, okay thanks. At least the news has been delivered to him and we can get straight to the questioning. That will save us some time.'

'Yes, ma'am,' Jenna said.

In Lauren's experience, speaking to the friend of a victim could be as traumatic, and sometimes worse, as when informing the family. It required finding a delicate balance between empathy and the need to gather information.

As they entered the interview room, Lauren's attention immediately homed in on the distraught figure hunched over the table. It was definitely the man who'd been in the jewellery shop with Finley Glenister.

Dylan Fairclough's eyes were red and puffy. He'd been crying and his hands shook as he fidgeted with the sleeve of his jumper.

'Thank you for coming in to see us, Dylan,' Lauren said as she and Jenna took their seats across from him. The plastic chairs creaked slightly and the sound was unnaturally loud in the silence of the room. 'We're going to record our chat.'

'Why?' he asked, his voice choked with emotion. His eyes darted between Lauren and Jenna, a flicker of fear crossing his face.

'It's easier that way and means we can concentrate on our conversation rather than taking notes.' Lauren nodded for Jenna to start the recording equipment and once they were underway, she returned her attention to him. 'We're very sorry for your loss; we understand that you and Finley were very close.'

'Yeah, I can't believe that he's dead. And Jasmine too. I was with them both on Saturday and they seemed so happy.' Fairclough's voice cracked as he began to speak again. 'I can't get my head around the idea that they would have... you know... killed themselves.' He looked down, blinking rapidly.

Lauren observed him carefully, noting every nuance of his body language. He was distressed but was there something else? Guilt? Fear? She couldn't be sure yet.

'Who told you that was how they died?' Lauren asked, making eye contact with the young man, but keeping her tone non-confrontational.

'Faith. As soon as I'd heard from the police, I messaged her. She replied and asked me if I knew that's what they'd planned to do.' He paused, swallowing hard. 'I didn't. I had no idea that things had got that bad. Fin didn't tell me...' He shook his head, his eyes pleading for them to believe him.

'Have you been in contact with Faith since then?'

'No...' He paused, appearing puzzled. 'Why?'

'I'm sorry to tell you that we're now treating Finley and Jasmine's deaths as suspicious.'

'What? So... you're now saying that they didn't kill themselves?' Fairclough paled, his hands gripping the edge of the table.

'Not according to the pathologist's report. What did you talk about when you last saw Finley and Jasmine on Saturday?' Lauren asked him, her eyes fixed on his.

'Um... nothing in particular. The three of us went to a bar at lunchtime. We had a laugh and talked about going back to uni. And other stuff. Nothing important... I can't really remember. Later in the evening we texted each other a bit.' Fairclough's eyes darted around the room, not settling on any one spot for long.

'When you say "we", do you mean you and Finley?' Lauren pressed, leaning forward slightly.

Fairclough nodded, his eyes darting between Lauren and Jenna. 'Yeah, that's right. Me and Fin.'

'What were you texting about?' Lauren asked, her gaze sharp.

'Making arrangements to meet up in the week. We've hardly seen each other recently because of my job.'

'What do you do?' Jenna asked.

Lauren started at the sound of Jenna's voice. Not because

she'd asked her not to speak, but she'd been quiet so far and Lauren had thought she was leaving the questioning to her. It often happened that a junior officer deferred to one more senior – other than in the case of when Lauren and Matt interviewed together. But theirs was a special relationship.

'I work at a bakery in Penzance,' Dylan responded.

'What can you tell us about the couple?' Lauren asked, refocusing the questioning. She folded her arms and rested them on the table.

'They've been going out together for a long time. They always seemed happy. I don't know what else to say... Um... people really liked them.' Fairclough's voice was flat, as if he was deliberately playing something down.

Why?

'We understand that Finley was a gambler. I assume you're aware of that?' Lauren asked.

Fairclough hesitated and glanced away. His shoulders were rigid and he appeared uncomfortable with the question.

Lauren waited for him to respond, letting the silence hang heavily in the air.

'Yes, you're right. Finley did gamble a lot,' Fairclough suddenly blurted. 'And... umm... You're going to find out anyway so I'll tell you – not that it matters now – he owed a lot of money.'

That was news to Lauren.

'We found some betting slips in his room. Is that what you mean? Did he owe the bookmakers?' she asked, tilting her head to one side.

'No. The slips would be from bets he'd placed and paid for. Bookies don't lend money to the likes of Fin.'

'Well, if he had debts, how could he afford to buy the ring?' Jenna asked, changing the subject.

Lauren had been about to follow up on the debts, but they

could revert back to that. She was interested in the engagement and the argument in the jewellery shop.

Fairclough shifted in his seat, his discomfort growing more apparent. 'I'm not sure. I asked him and he wouldn't tell me.'

Lauren's eyes narrowed. There was more here, she was sure of it. 'We've seen CCTV footage from the jewellery shop when Finley bought the engagement ring. You were there, too, weren't you?'

'Yes.' Fairclough's response was clipped and his body language closed off.

'We understand the two of you were arguing. You were telling Finley either not to buy the ring or not propose to Jasmine. The woman in the shop wasn't quite sure.'

Fairclough sighed heavily, running a hand through his hair. 'Look, I didn't tell Finley not to propose. I was suggesting that he leave it for a while. He owed too much money and I didn't think he should be paying for a ring that expensive. I said that he should pay off his debts before it got him into trouble.'

Lauren nodded encouragingly. 'What was his response?'

Fairclough's eyes glazed over a bit as if he was remembering the encounter. 'He said it was fine because he had a dead cert coming up and he'd make all the money he needed to pay off his debts.'

'Did you believe him?' Lauren asked.

'I guess...' Fairclough said.

'So what was this *dead cert*? A horse race?' Lauren asked.

'I don't know. He'd often bet on the horses but he also played poker online and sometimes won a lot of money.' Fairclough paused, looking down at his hands. His fingers were intertwined. 'That was the problem. He won quite a lot of money about eight months ago, and instead of using it to pay his debts, he ended up gambling it away. But he enjoyed the feeling of winning. Or at least that's what he told me when I had a go about it.'

Lauren frowned. This was becoming more and more concerning. A gambling addict, in debt, suddenly able to afford an expensive engagement ring. Where had the money come from?

'According to his parents, he'd got this problem under control,' she probed.

'He did stop for a while. Jasmine and I did a sort of intervention.'

'What do you mean?' Lauren had always assumed that interventions were what they did in the United States.

'We sat him down and told him we were going to be with him all the time during the day to stop him from making any bets.'

'What about the online betting? He could've done that when you weren't with him,' Lauren asked, already seeing the flaw in their approach.

'Yes, we realised that, which is why Jasmine took his laptop when we couldn't be with him.'

'What about his phone, couldn't he use that?' Jenna asked.

'We deleted the app and Jasmine regularly checked to make sure he hadn't downloaded it again.'

'So you thought of everything,' Lauren said with a sharp nod.

'We thought so until...' His voice trailed away.

'Until what?' Lauren pushed.

'Once the gambling had stopped, we eased up on the intervention because he promised that he wouldn't start again. That was a mistake.' Fairclough's voice was little more than a whisper.

'Tell us what happened,' Lauren urged, wanting to know the complete story.

'He started again. I'm not sure what set him off but I do know he borrowed money to finance it.'

'How recently did the gambling resume?' Lauren asked,

wondering if this was going to somehow fit in with their timeline.

'A couple of months ago.'

'Who loaned him the money?' Lauren asked.

'A guy at uni,' Fairclough replied, with a shrug. 'Alfie Hackett.'

Lauren made a mental note of the name. A new lead. 'Is he a friend?'

'Not really. We'd see him around in the student bars, but didn't hang out with him. I'm not sure how Fin got to borrow money from him.'

'Are you sure?' Lauren pushed. 'You were his best friend, so surely he'd tell you.'

'Fin kept secrets from everyone,' Fairclough said with a shrug.

'How did you find out, then?' Lauren asked.

'Fin confided in me when he couldn't afford to pay Hackett back. Hackett had threatened him and he was scared. He wanted me to back him up if it came to anything.'

'Did you witness any of these threats?' Lauren asked, her voice intense.

'No, Fin told me.' Fairclough's eyes were wide, almost fearful.

'Yet he still bought the ring, even after he knew Hackett was going to come after him?'

'Yes, and that's why I wanted him not to,' Fairclough said, nodding miserably.

'That makes no sense.'

Lauren tapped her fingers on the desk, mulling over what they'd learnt. A desperate gambler, in debt to a loan shark who was pressuring him. It certainly provided a potential motive. But for murder? That still seemed extreme.

'A lot of what Fin did didn't make sense. That was just him,' Fairclough said, with a resigned sigh.

'What can you tell me about Alfie Hackett?' Lauren asked, her voice carefully impartial.

'Nothing other than he lives in Barnstaple.'

'I see. Do you believe that Hackett was capable of harming Finley and Jasmine because of this?' Lauren asked.

'No way. That's crazy. First of all, Jasmine wasn't involved. She hadn't borrowed money from him. And why would Hackett murder them? There would be no point. He'd never get his money back then, would he?' Fairclough's voice rose slightly, a note of desperation creeping in.

'Well, sometimes these things happen as a warning to others,' Lauren said carefully. She observed Fairclough's face closely, looking for any sign of deception. 'Is there anything else you can think of that might assist us in finding out what happened to Finley and Jasmine?'

'Nothing,' Fairclough said, tears filling his eyes. 'I can't believe it. We've been friends for years. We went to school together, and then university.'

'How come you didn't go travelling with them to Australia and New Zealand?' Jenna asked.

'I really wanted to but at the time I needed to work to get some money saved for uni.' He swiped at his eyes. 'I wish I had gone with them. They told me it was awesome over there.'

'That's all for now, thank you,' Lauren said. 'We're very sorry for your loss. It must be very difficult for you. Would you like someone to take you home?'

'No thanks. I'm going to work.'

Lauren's eyebrows shot up in surprise. 'Even after all this?'

'Yeah. Finley's family gave him everything he wanted, but mine don't. I'll be sacked if I let them down. I'm on the later afternoon/evening shift today. I prefer to do those hours because I get unsociable hours rate.'

Lauren stood up, her chair scraping against the floor.

'Remember to let us know if there's anything else you think of that might help,' she repeated.

They escorted Fairclough to the front door and then headed back to the office. Lauren's mind was whirling with the new information. Hackett was a promising lead. A potentially dangerous man with a clear grievance against Finley Glenister. But, as Jenna and Fairclough had pointed out, why kill someone who owed you money? Unless…

'Ma'am?' Jenna interrupted her thoughts. 'What do you think?'

Lauren sighed, running a hand through her hair. 'We need to speak to Alfie Hackett and get his perspective.'

'But, as we've already discussed, why kill someone if they owe you money? It makes no sense.'

'I agree, but what we must consider, as I said to Fairclough, is that it can be as a warning to others. If Hackett regularly lends money, he might consider it collateral damage.' Lauren grimaced. 'It wouldn't be the first time I've come across something like this.'

'Oh,' Jenna said, with a nod.

Lauren flashed back to a case early in her career when a young man had been beaten to death over a drug debt of a few hundred pounds. Senseless brutality, all for the sake of sending a message. Lauren had learnt then that there was no limit to the violence some people were capable of. If Hackett was that type of man…

She shook her head, trying to clear the dark memories. It was best for them not to jump to conclusions. They needed facts and evidence.

'Okay,' she said decisively. 'We need an address for Hackett and then we'll pay him a visit. It's a six-hour round trip to Barnstaple, so we'll go first thing tomorrow morning.'

Lauren returned to her office and leant back in her chair, her eyes drifting to the photocopied photos of Finley and

Jasmine on her desk. They were both smiling and appearing hopeful; their whole lives were ahead of them. Except their lives had been cut tragically short.

She picked up Finley's photo and studied his face. What secrets had he been hiding? What desperate measures had he been driven to? And had someone decided that his life, and Jasmine's, were worth less than a gambling debt?

TWELVE

MONDAY 11 SEPTEMBER

There was a tap on Lauren's door and Clem stuck his head around.

'Ma'am, the key found on Jasmine Dodd has arrived. Do you want to open the box in here?' He held out the key.

'No, I'll come out so we can view the contents together.' Lauren closed the report she'd been writing, picked up the evidence bag containing the box, which was on the filing cabinet, and headed into the office.

Clem passed over the small brass key to Lauren and she examined it in her gloved hands before sliding it into the lock of the raffia box. It fitted perfectly and the mechanism clicked as she turned it. Inside were several envelopes.

She pulled one out, opened it and began to read out loud. '"Jas, I watch you with Finley every day and it kills me. You deserve so much better than him. I know you don't see it yet, but we'd be perfect together. The way you smiled at me in the library yesterday had to mean something."' Lauren paused, looking up at the team. 'It's signed "love Dylan".'

'Dylan Fairclough?' Billy said. 'Finley's best mate?'

'Who else can it be?' Lauren spread out the envelopes

across the table and picked up another. "'I know you're happy with Finley, but he doesn't appreciate you like I do. He didn't even notice your new haircut last week, but I did. I notice everything about you. Sometimes I catch you looking at me and I think maybe you feel it too...'"

'There's something distinctly creepy about this,' Jenna said. 'What do the others say?'

Lauren opened another. "'I saw you kiss him outside the lecture hall today and I had to leave. Don't you understand what you're doing to me? Every time you touch him it should be me. It's like you're trying to hurt me on purpose.'"

'Why would she keep letters from her boyfriend's best friend confessing his feelings? That's the kind of thing that could destroy friendships,' Jenna said.

'Maybe she kept them as evidence. These aren't love letters... they're becoming increasingly obsessive. She wanted to document it in case things escalated. Smart girl,' Lauren replied.

'Except she's still dead,' Billy added, his comment leaving a chill in the air.

'True,' Jenna said, nodding.

'I wonder if Jasmine responded,' Lauren mused. 'Maybe her friend Ruby will know.'

'Shall we bring him back in?' Clem asked.

Lauren stared at the letters, each one a documentation of obsession growing darker. 'No,' she said finally. 'Let's gather more evidence first. When we interview him again, I want all of our ducks in a row. Billy you've been looking into him. What have you discovered?'

'Actually, ma'am, there is something, which I'd been about to share before we got the key. It's definitely relevant.'

Lauren stared directly at the officer, anxious to hear what he had to say. 'Let's hear it.'

'I spoke to the headteacher at Dylan Fairclough's old school in Penzance and in his final year there was a complaint made against him by one of the female teachers. Eva Millington. It seems he had an infatuation with her and took it too far,' Billy reported, his voice carrying a note of triumph.

'In what way?'

'He sent her flowers and left gifts for her in her pigeonhole. He also followed her home and stood outside her house staring.'

Lauren's stomach flipped. She could picture vividly the teacher's growing unease. The way she might have started checking over her shoulder on her way home, perhaps changing her routine.

'Did it go any further? Did he make any unwarranted approaches?' Lauren asked, hoping in a way that he had because it was all evidence of his obsessive nature getting out of control. Although she was mindful of the subtle terror it would have caused Eva Millington.

'No. His parents were called to the school and he was threatened with suspension if he continued the behaviour.'

'Did it stop after that?'

'Yes, it did. He sent a written apology to the teacher,' Billy said.

Was the written apology based on genuine remorse, or another way to be in contact with the teacher?

'Ma'am, do you think this started after Jasmine began seeing Finley?' Jenna asked. 'Maybe he transferred his feelings for her onto this teacher.'

The question sent a jolt through Lauren. It was exactly what she'd been thinking.

'We'll ask him. Do we know what this teacher looks like?'

'Hang on a minute, ma'am,' Billy said. 'She still teaches there so I'll call up the school website.'

The silence that followed was heavy with anticipation and Lauren found herself holding her breath, her eyes fixed on Billy as he tapped on his keyboard.

'Bloody hell,' he said after a minute of searching.

'What is it?' Lauren asked, realising that he'd uncovered something important.

'This teacher's a dead ringer for Jasmine. Dainty features, with blonde hair framing her face.'

Lauren hurried over to Billy's desk to take a look at the image on his screen. A chill ran down her spine as she studied the photo. This wasn't just evidence of Dylan's obsessive behaviour; it illustrated a pattern.

'Thanks, Billy.' She turned to face the rest of the team. 'Remember, everyone, this isn't incriminating in itself, but we can use it when questioning Dylan Fairclough.' She paused while thinking through her next steps. 'We need to speak to Eva Millington. School is over for the day, so we'll interview her tomorrow on our way back from visiting Alfie Hackett.'

The energy of the room had shifted as the team processed what they'd now gleaned about Dylan Fairclough. If he'd been obsessed with Jasmine and then transferred it to Eva Millington and then back again, they were dealing with a complex process and one which needed careful handling.

THIRTEEN

TUESDAY 12 SEPTEMBER

Matt sucked in a deep breath, pausing outside the entrance to the station as the familiar building loomed before him. Even though he'd only been away for a day, it seemed like an eternity. The image of his father in the hospital bed, pale and weak, flashed in front of his eyes, but he pushed it aside. His dad was holding his own, and hopefully that would continue. The doctors had said that it was a warning, which in a way had to be a good thing. At least now they could do something about it. If he'd had a full-blown stroke and not a mini one then goodness knows what would have happened.

With a final steadying breath, Matt pushed open the glass double doors and stepped into the bustling station. The familiar sounds and smells washed over him: the low hum of conversation, the rhythmic tapping of keyboards on the front desk, and the constant ringing of the phone. It was oddly comforting, a slice of normality in the chaos his life had so quickly become.

He headed directly to the main office but no one else had arrived. The room seemed eerily quiet without the usual banter and activity of his team. He could see the outline of Lauren's head through the frosted glass of her office and, squaring his shoulders, he went over and knocked.

'Morning, ma'am,' he said, poking his head around the door.

The sight of Lauren, bent over a stack of papers, her brow furrowed in concentration, was reassuringly familiar.

Lauren's head snapped up, surprise evident in her eyes. 'Matt. What are you doing here? How's your dad?'

Matt stepped fully into the office, closing the door behind him. 'He's okay, thanks. It was confirmed to be a TIA. Transient ischaemic attack. It's like a mini-stroke, which is more of a warning really, but he's still in the hospital. Obviously, things must change in terms of his lifestyle, but we've got time to work it out.'

Lauren nodded sympathetically, her eyes softening. 'I didn't think he had a particularly bad lifestyle.'

Matt sank into the chair opposite Lauren's desk. 'It's things like his diet. You know my mum, she's always making cakes and desserts. Too much sugar. He's got to eat a lot more unprocessed food.'

'That can't be a bad thing. I'm glad that he's doing okay. Please send him my best wishes when you visit. But you really don't need to be here.'

Matt appreciated her worry, but he knew work was exactly where he should be. 'Yes, I do. Can you give me an update on where we are?'

'Okay, but remember if it gets too much, or if you're called away, just go. We'll manage. Regarding what you've missed. I've literally just had a message from Henry saying that despite the families providing samples of Jasmine and Finley's handwriting, they couldn't accurately discern whether either of them wrote the note.'

'That doesn't surprise me when you think that there were only five letters and they were all in caps. Anything else?'

'Yes. Ellie went through the victims' mobile phones

yesterday and there was nothing in there that alerted us to anything untoward happening.' Lauren sat up straighter in her chair and gave a smile. 'Now for the interesting stuff. Dylan Fairclough, Finley Glenister's best friend, told us about his friend's extensive gambling debts. He owes money to a fellow student, Alfie Hackett. But, more importantly, we've since learnt that Fairclough was infatuated with Jasmine Dodd and has a history of obsessive behaviour. In his final year, he was threatened with suspension from school for stalking Eva Millington, a teacher there.'

'Wow,' Matt said. 'Have you spoken to her yet?'

'No, I'd originally planned to go after interviewing Hackett, who lives in Barnstaple. But I realised last night that we might not make it back before school finishes for the day so we'll go there first. I was going to take Jenna but you can come with me instead.' She paused a moment, clearly deliberating. 'Actually, it's going to be a long day, so maybe you won't want to.'

'I do. I'll let Mum know I might be late home. Dani's at nursery, and she can collect her later. Like I said, my dad's not in any danger now.'

Lauren studied him for a moment, her eyes searching his face. Matt met her gaze steadily, willing her to see his determination. Finally, she nodded.

'Well, if you're sure. Certainly, I'd rather have you with me. Jenna's done very well and has asked some perceptive questions, but you're more observant, and can think outside the box. I've already phoned the school to let them know we'll be there around nine-thirty.'

'Thanks. I need to sort out a couple of things and then I'll be back.' He turned to leave and then looked back at her. 'By the way, how are Ben and Tia after their ordeal?'

'They're fine, thanks for asking,' Lauren said, giving a dismissive wave of her hand. 'They didn't even realise there was anything wrong. Other than they had a shorter than usual walk on Sunday. I asked Betty from next door to check on them more regularly than usual, in case, but she said they were no different from how they always are.'

'Well, that's good,' Matt replied with a smile. 'You're lucky to have Betty close by.'

'Don't I know it. She's been talking about selling up and moving closer to her daughter, but I hope she doesn't. Does that make me mean?' Lauren shrugged slightly.

'Not at all. But it does make one realise that we need others around us.'

He returned to the office at the same time that Jenna and Clem arrived.

'Hi, Sarge,' Jenna said brightly, her smile warm. 'How's your dad?'

'He's fine and doing all right, thanks, which is why I'm back at work. I can't hang around doing nothing.'

'I'm so glad to hear that,' Jenna said sincerely. 'There's nothing worse than your parents getting old and you having to deal with things that happen.' She paused, glancing towards Lauren's office. 'I take it you'll be accompanying the DI today?'

'Yes, we've been discussing it.'

'Ah, well, that's great,' she said, letting out an obvious sigh of relief.

Matt frowned, picking up on her odd tone. 'What's the problem, Jenna?'

She coloured slightly. 'Oh, it's nothing. I mean, I did want to go. It's just that... I don't know... the DI might have changed for the better since you've been here, Sarge, but even so. Spending hours in the car together could be awkward, if you get what I mean.'

Matt couldn't help but smile at Jenna's discomfort. Lauren could be intimidating, especially for less senior officers. But there was no one he'd rather have by his side on a case like this.

'Well, you don't need to worry about that now,' he reassured the officer.

'Thanks, Sarge. I appreciate it.'

She hurried off to her desk and Matt sat at his own. He checked through his emails, answering those that were important, leaving the rest for another time. It was already gone nine and they needed to get moving.

He grabbed his jacket from the coat stand in the corner of the room and headed for Lauren's office. A flicker of excitement, alongside the determination that always accompanied a murder case, coursed through him. With the exception of Dani, this was what he lived for. The thrill of the chase, the satisfaction of putting the pieces together and seeing justice served.

He knocked on Lauren's door and entered at her call. She was standing by the desk, her bag already over her shoulder, and met his eyes with a determined smile.

'You ready?' Lauren asked.

Matt nodded. 'Yeah. Let's go and see what Eva Millington has to tell us.'

FOURTEEN

TUESDAY 12 SEPTEMBER

Lauren drummed her fingers on the steering wheel as they drove towards the school in Penzance where Eva Millington worked. The morning was bright but cool, typical for early autumn in Cornwall, with seabirds wheeling overhead against a powder-blue sky.

'I've arranged for us to go to the school office and they'll fetch her,' Lauren said, breaking the comfortable silence.

'What do we know about her?' Matt asked.

'According to Billy, she's been at the school for eight years and teaches English. The office administrator whom I spoke to was going to inform her that we're on our way. I explained that there was nothing for the teacher to worry about.'

'Good,' Matt responded. 'People are always on edge as soon as they know we want to speak to them.'

The satnav directed them to turn off the main road, and soon they were navigating narrow lanes bordered by ancient Cornish stone walls. The school appeared ahead of them. It was a sprawling mix of Victorian architecture and modern extensions, surrounded by well-maintained playing fields.

Their footsteps echoed in the empty corridor as they

followed the signs to the school office. They made their introductions and the administrator escorted them to an empty classroom close by to wait.

After a few minutes Eva Millington walked in. The resemblance to Jasmine was uncanny, even more so than the photo they saw on the website. The same delicate features, the same honey-blonde hair framing her face. Eva was older, late thirties to Jasmine's early twenties, but they could easily have been sisters.

'Detective Inspector Pengelly,' Lauren introduced herself, showing her warrant card. 'This is Detective Sergeant Price. Thank you for agreeing to meet with us, Eva. Please sit down.' Lauren gestured to the three chairs that she'd arranged into an informal triangle next to the desk at the front, making the space feel friendlier, less like a classroom.

Eva's smile was polite but stiff. 'I've been told you want to discuss Dylan Fairclough.' The woman's fingers twisted together as she said his name, a subtle tell that the memories still held power.

'Yes, a pattern has emerged in our current case that makes your experience with Dylan particularly relevant.'

Eva's shoulders stiffened slightly. 'He's done it again, hasn't he? I'm not surprised,' she said quietly, meeting Lauren's gaze directly. 'What do you want to know?'

'Please go through what happened,' Matt asked, his notebook ready.

Eva ran a hand through her hair and sighed. It still appeared painful for her.

'Take your time,' Lauren added, wanting to put the woman at her ease.

'Thank you. It started small.' Her gaze turned distant as she remembered. 'He was always eager to participate in class discussions, especially when we were studying romantic literature. At first, I was pleased. I mean, you don't get many boys of his age willing to analyse authors like Jane Austen in such detail.' A bitter smile crossed her face. 'I didn't realise he was drawing parallels between himself and the romantic heroes we'd discussed.'

Lauren leant forward slightly. 'When did you first notice his behaviour becoming inappropriate?'

'It was gradual. He started staying behind after class to ask questions, which isn't unusual in itself because students do. But after a while the questions became more personal and less about what we were studying. He'd ask about my weekend plans and my favourite books. He also asked whether I enjoyed living alone.' Eva paused, glancing up nervously.

'How did he know that?' Matt asked, looking up from his notebook.

'I don't know, but it's not something I've ever hidden. I may have mentioned it in class some time. I really can't remember.' She sighed again. 'Anyway, then the gifts started appearing in my pigeonhole. Nothing expensive. Chocolates, books, and once a single red rose. Each came with a note analysing my teaching style or commenting on something I'd said in class and thanking me for making the subject interesting.'

'Did you confront him about it?' Matt asked.

'I didn't want to get him in trouble so spoke to him privately, to establish proper boundaries. He seemed to understand and appeared genuinely apologetic. Everything seemed okay for a while but then   ' She stopped, her hands clenching into fists on the desk.

'Take your time,' Lauren said softly.

'I started noticing him outside my house. At first, I thought it was coincidence. Penzance isn't that big, after all. But he was there every evening, standing across the street, watching. Sometimes for hours. If I opened the curtains, he'd wave, as if it was perfectly normal.' Eva's voice shook slightly. 'The worst part was, he never did anything threatening. He was always perfectly polite, even when he was terrifying me.'

This pattern of escalating obsession matched perfectly with their current case. 'What made you finally report it?'

'One night, I came home late from a school concert. It was pouring with rain and he was standing there, soaked to the skin. He said he wanted to make sure I got home safely. That's when I realised how dangerous the situation had become. I reported it to the head teacher and his parents were called in.'

'And after that?' Lauren asked.

'The physical stalking stopped. He wrote me an apology letter that was...' Eva hesitated, appearing to choose her words carefully. 'It was simultaneously one of the sincerest and most disturbing things I've ever read. He compared himself to Heathcliff from *Wuthering Heights* and said that like him, he would learn to channel his passionate nature into more acceptable forms of expression.' She gave a hollow laugh.

'Do you still have the letter?' Lauren asked.

'Yes. It's at home. It felt important, somehow. I must have had a premonition that it might be needed as evidence in the future.'

Lauren sat up straighter. 'Would you be willing to share it with us? It could be valuable to our investigation.'

Eva nodded immediately. 'Of course. I can get it for you now if you'd like. I only live ten minutes away.'

'That would be extremely helpful,' Lauren said. 'We'll go in my car.'

Eva's cottage was a traditional Cornish stone building with granite walls softened by age and weather. A small front garden was bordered by weathered wooden posts linked by iron chains. The garden itself was a carefully maintained mix of cottage flowers and herbs. Lauren spotted lavender, rosemary, and what looked like sage pushing up through the soil.

'I won't be a moment,' Eva said, jumping out of the car and disappearing inside.

'The similarity really is remarkable, ma'am.'

'I know,' Lauren replied. 'But whom did he fixate on first? We need to discover if once Jasmine got together with Finley, he transferred his affections onto the teacher. Or whether it was the reverse and because of what happened with the teacher he moved on to Jasmine.'

Eva returned quickly, clutching a white envelope that had appeared to have been handled many times over the years. 'Here it is. I hope it helps.'

Lauren accepted the envelope carefully. 'Thank you, Eva. You've been extremely helpful. We'll need to take a formal statement at some point, but this is an excellent start.'

They dropped off the teacher at the school and as Lauren drove away, she caught sight of Eva's reflection in the rearview mirror. A solitary figure at the entrance, her arms wrapped around herself.

'Barnstaple next, ma'am?' Matt asked.

Lauren's fingers tightened on the steering wheel. 'Yes, Mr Hackett first. Then we deal with Dylan Fairclough.'

FIFTEEN

TUESDAY 12 SEPTEMBER

Lauren drove them towards Barnstaple and, speeding along the A30, Matt was struck by the distinct changes from the rocky coastline of Cornwall to the rolling hills of Devon.

He turned to Lauren, deciding to voice the question that had been nagging at him since they'd left Penzance. 'Why didn't you think about doing the interview on the phone, ma'am? What if this all amounts to nothing?'

Lauren took a sharp breath. 'I disagree; I hardly think it's going to be nothing. We have two victims, one of whom owed money to Hackett. It's going to be worth it.' Her tone left no room for argument. 'Are you asking because you're regretting coming with me because of your dad?' she asked, her tone softening slightly.

She was right. He hadn't anticipated there being a problem, but the further away they were from Cornwall the more he worried that something might happen to his father and he wouldn't be able to make a mad dash over to Truro hospital. He really hadn't thought it through properly.

'Well, maybe a little because of the long drive,' Matt admitted. 'But I'm sure it will be fine.'

He stared out the window at the rolling green hills, which were dotted with sheep and cattle, that stretched out before them under a cloudy sky. The pastoral scene seemed at odds with the bleak nature of their journey.

'Try not to worry. If anything happens, I promise we'll head right back to the hospital with the siren blaring,' Lauren said, smiling.

'Thanks.'

They drove in silence for a while, Matt's thoughts drifting to his dad and how their lives were going to change. He'd need rest and quiet but how was that going to happen with a small child bounding around? Matt would have to figure out a plan.

The further north they drove the more the scenery changed, especially when they passed the craggy terrain of Bodmin Moor. Every so often they'd pass through a quaint village of stone cottages huddled around a central green.

Nearer to the north coast, the landscape gave way to a patchwork of fields and hedgerows. The narrow lanes twisted and turned, flanked by tall banks dripping with ferns and wildflowers. Matt opened his window slightly and breathed in the damp, earthy scent of the Devon countryside. Some of the tension left his shoulders.

But despite the picturesque surroundings, his thoughts kept drifting back to his dad lying in the hospital bed, so different from how alert and strong he usually was. He couldn't imagine his dad not being around. Even though he knew that one day it was going to happen, he wasn't ready for it yet.

'Hey, your dad's a fighter. He'll pull through this.' Lauren reached over and squeezed his arm.

Matt managed a strained smile in return, grateful for her support.

He stared out at the road ahead, trying to pull back his spiralling thoughts to the case as the outskirts of Barnstaple came into view. It was a pleasant location, and Matt appreciated the scenery as they passed by the river. He admired the colourful boats bobbing in the quay and the Victorian architecture of the houses that lined the riverbank. It was a welcome distraction.

'What's our game plan for Hackett?' he asked.

Lauren glanced at him, a determined glint in her eye. 'I think it's best if we play it cool so we don't put him on his guard. He won't be surprised that he's being interviewed because of the loan he made to Finley Glenister – assuming he knows of the death. Initially, we'll ask him about his relationship with the victims and how much money he'd loaned. Then we'll move on to where he was on the night of the murders.'

Matt nodded, jotting down notes. 'And if he's not cooperative?'

'Then we push harder,' Lauren said firmly. 'One way or another, we're going to discover if Hackett's involved in the murders.'

Alfie Hackett lived with his parents in a large modern property on a small development at the edge of town. They pulled into the drive and Matt took in the manicured lawn and the shiny BMW parked in front of the garage.

Lauren parked and they marched to the front door. Matt rang the bell and a young man who appeared to be Alfie Hackett, based on the photos they'd seen of him, answered. He was tall and well-built, with an air of confidence that seemed to falter slightly at the sight of them.

'Mr Hackett?' Lauren asked, holding out her warrant card.

'Yes?' Hackett replied warily.

'I'm DI Pengelly and this is DS Price from Penzance police. We'd like a word with you, please.'

'Why?' Hackett asked, his brow furrowed in confusion. His eyes darted between them, a flicker of unease crossing his face.

Maybe he wasn't aware that Glenister had died.

'Can we speak inside?' Lauren asked, her tone making it sound more like an order then a question.

'Who is it, Alfie?' A female voice came from behind him. The woman who appeared was smartly dressed in a pair of wide-legged navy trousers and a pale pink striped shirt over a white T-shirt. Her dark auburn hair was neatly pulled back from her face, held in place by a black headband. There was certainly a family resemblance and Matt assumed it was Alfie Hackett's mother.

'Mrs Hackett?' Lauren asked.

'Yes.'

'We're here to have a word with Alfie regarding one of the people he knows at university, if we may.'

Matt frowned. He was surprised at Lauren being so forthright to the man's mother. He was over eighteen and she wasn't responsible for him. Then again, they had decided to play it down and this would ensure everyone's cooperation.

'Why? What's happened?' Mrs Hackett looked between them, her features growing more concerned.

'We can't discuss this with anyone other than your son. But it's nothing for you to worry about.'

'I see. In that case, why don't you take the officers into the snug, Alfie,' Mrs Hackett said with a nod, turning to her son.

'Yes, Mum.' He opened the door more fully and ushered them in. 'It's through here.'

They followed him into a small room, and Matt closed the door behind them. There were two tan leather sofas facing each other and a coffee table in between, with several large books in the centre. Various photos stood on an oak sideboard and some artwork hung on the walls. The room was tastefully decorated, but the photos had an impersonal feel, like they belonged to a show home rather than a lived-in space.

Hackett sat on one sofa while Matt and Lauren took the other. Matt's eyes were drawn to Hackett's right knee, which was bouncing up and down. Nerves? Was it because he had something to hide, or simply the fact that the police wanted to talk to him? People often froze in their presence, even if they weren't guilty of anything.

'We understand you know Finley Glenister?' Lauren began, her tone neutral.

'Yes, unfortunately.' Hackett shifted in his seat, appearing to look everywhere except directly at them.

'Both Finley and his girlfriend, Jasmine Dodd, have recently died.'

Hackett's jaw dropped open. 'What? I had no idea. I...' He voice petered out and he stared blankly ahead.

His shock certainly seemed genuine enough, but Matt knew better than to take that at face value. Some offenders would swear on their families' lives that red was white if they thought it would get them off.

'It hasn't been publicised yet,' Lauren said. 'I'd like to return to your relationship with Finley and Jasmine. How well did you know them?'

'I knew Finley quite well, I suppose.'

'How did you meet him?'

'We met at a party and got on well.'

Hackett fidgeted with his hands in his lap. His nerves seemed to be getting worse. Was he anticipating where the interview was heading?

'How did it go from there to you lending Finley Glenister money?' Matt asked pointedly.

Hackett peered over his shoulder as if not wanting anyone to overhear. 'We were in the student bar one evening and he was complaining about having no money. I offered to lend him some if he ever needed any.'

'How much?' Matt asked.

'Twice he borrowed two thousand pounds and the last time it was twenty thousand.'

'Where do you get the money from to lend?' Lauren asked, frowning.

'I have savings. My grandparents left me some in their will last year.' Hackett shrugged nonchalantly as if it was no big deal.

'When you lent him money, how much interest did you charge?' Lauren asked.

Hackett coloured slightly and stared directly ahead.

'Alfie, please answer the DI's question?' Matt pushed.

'Fifty percent,' Hackett muttered.

Lauren raised an eyebrow. 'Wow. You were lending thousands of pounds at fifty percent interest? That's not a bad return on your money.'

'Only if you get it back,' Hackett snapped.

'Does that mean he didn't pay you back?' Lauren asked.

'Usually he did, but the last time he didn't.'

'I take it you were annoyed with him about that,' Lauren pressed.

'Of course I was. I needed the money. It wasn't a gift.' Hackett's tone had turned defensive.

'Do you know why he borrowed the money?'

'He's a gambler. The first time I lent him money he told me he'd got himself into debt. I assumed it was the same for the other loans. His reasons were nothing to do with me.'

'Did Finley accept your offer straight away? Even after you told him the interest rate?' Matt asked, trying to hide his annoyance that Hackett took advantage of Finley Glenister in this way.

'Pretty much, yeah. He was desperate for the money and didn't care about the interest.'

'Did you sign a contract?' Matt asked, his gaze unwavering.

Hackett rolled his eyes and his lips curled up in a sneer. 'What do you think?' he said flatly.

'Okay, I get it,' Matt said, pinching the bridge of his nose. 'Did you tell anyone about the loan?'

'No, we kept it between the two of us.'

Matt leant forward. 'What were you doing on Saturday night between the hours of nine pm and midnight?'

'I was at the Red Lion pub with my friends. Why?'

'Can any of them confirm that?' Matt asked, ignoring the man's question.

'Well, we sort of got split up. I was talking to a girl but I don't remember her name.' Hackett shrugged.

Lauren made a note. 'That's a pretty weak alibi. So no one at this pub will recall you being there?'

'I'm not sure.' Hackett appeared increasingly uncomfortable. 'But why does it matter?'

'We're treating the deaths of Finley and Jasmine as suspicious.'

'Oh...' Hackett's body stiffened and his muscles visibly tensed.

'I'm surprised you didn't ask us how they died,' Lauren said. 'Why not?'

'Umm... I don't know. I was too shocked, I suppose.'

'Have you ever been prescribed sleeping medication?' Lauren asked.

'No. Why?'

'What about any of your family?' Lauren pushed.

'I don't know. Why are you asking?' Hackett said, appearing confused.

'Who else do you lend money to?' Matt asked, shifting the direction of the interview.

'No one on a regular basis apart from Finley.'

Matt and Lauren exchanged a meaningful glance. The same thought passing wordlessly between them. Hackett's 'lending' sounded like illegal loan sharking, with Glenister as his main client. But did the large sum Glenister owed provide a compelling motive for murder?

'Right. We'd like to have a look at your bedroom.' Lauren stood and Matt did the same.

'Why?' Hackett's voice rose, a note of panic creeping in.

'If you've got nothing to hide, you won't mind,' Lauren responded, not bothering to answer his question.

'Okay,' the man said begrudgingly.

Hackett led the way upstairs and stood in the doorway while Matt and Lauren went inside. The room was a stark contrast to the impersonal neatness of the rest of the house. Clothes, textbooks and art supplies cluttered every surface. The walls were covered in sketches and designs.

'What are you studying at university?'

'Textile design,' Hackett said with a shrug.

Lauren picked up a sketchpad from the desk and started flicking through it. Her eyes widened. 'These sketches are all of Faith Glenister, Finley's younger sister. Why didn't you tell us that you know her?' She held out the detailed portraits of Faith for Matt to see.

A flush crept up Hackett's neck. 'You didn't ask.'

'So explain,' Lauren demanded.

'There's nothing to say. She was out with her brother and his friends one night and we got talking.'

'Does Faith know about your feelings for her?' Matt pushed.

'I'm not sure. Probably not. I think she views me as a friend,' Hackett mumbled, casting his eyes to the floor.

'Did Faith let you know what had happened to her brother and his girlfriend?' Matt pressed further.

'No.'

'So when you say *friend* she's more like an acquaintance?' Matt pushed, trying to get to the bottom of their relationship.

'Well, yes, I suppose so,' Hackett admitted.

'We need to check your alibi and will be contacting the Red

Lion, to see if anyone can vouch for you being there on Saturday night,' Lauren said crisply.

After ending the interview, Matt mulled over Hackett's unrequited feelings for Faith. Combined with the revelation of his loan sharking and the flimsy alibi, he was looking more and more like a solid suspect. But they still needed hard evidence to link him definitively to the murders.

Once they'd returned to the car, Lauren faced him. 'Well, Hackett's got motive, for sure.'

'Agreed. And opportunity. But no murder weapon or forensics yet.' Matt rubbed a hand along his chin. 'We need to dig more into his background and confirm his alibi. He knows more than he's letting on.'

After Lauren pulled away from the house and joined the traffic, Matt took out his phone to message his mum. The knot in his chest eased slightly when he saw she'd already texted him. *Dad sitting up and eating a sandwich. He sends his love.*

Matt breathed a sigh of relief and typed a quick response to say what time he thought he'd be home.

They fell into a comfortable silence and Matt found himself drifting off to sleep, unable to keep his eyes open.

'Matt... Matt... we're here.' He could hear his boss's voice but for a second forgot where he was.

'Sorry, ma'am. I didn't get much sleep last night,' he said with a weary smile.

'No need to apologise. I totally understand,' Lauren said as she pulled up beside his car in the station car park. 'Give my best wishes to your dad – and try to get some rest. We've got a long day ahead of us tomorrow.'

SIXTEEN

WEDNESDAY 13 SEPTEMBER

Lauren sat at the table, watching the early morning light creep across her kitchen table. The half-finished cardigan she was knitting for Matt's daughter, Dani, lay beside her breakfast plate, its soft yellow wool catching the sun. She'd chosen the colour carefully, wanting it to be perfect for the little girl who was slowly becoming part of her life, though now she wondered if she should have gone with the mint green instead.

Something was niggling at the edges of her consciousness. What if there had been another creditor, someone a lot nastier than Hackett? Someone whose method of debt collection culminated in murder. She'd need to get Ellie to dig deeper, check the less obvious channels.

Lauren looked at her watch, quickly downed the last of her coffee and let the dogs out for a quick run in the garden. As she gathered her things, her fingers brushed against the soft wool of Dani's cardigan. The simple act of creating something, stitch by stitch, had always helped her think.

When she arrived at the station the night shift was winding down and bleary-faced officers nodded to her on their way out.

She made her way to her office and, before settling at her

desk, took a moment to survey the larger room beyond the open door. The whiteboard dominated one side covered in photos, timelines and scrawled notes. But so far nothing had gelled.

Sighing, she turned to her computer and began sifting through the emails that had accumulated during her absence yesterday. The soft hum of the machine and the gentle tapping of her keyboard were the only sounds in the quiet office.

Suddenly, the shrill ring of her phone shattered the early morning calm. Lauren reached for it, her heartbeat quickening with anticipation.

'Pengelly,' she answered, her voice crisp and professional even though it was very early.

'Morning, Inspector.'

Lauren immediately recognised the pathologist's voice on the other end of the line.

'Good morning, Henry. What have you got for me?' She leant forward, grabbing a pen and notepad, ready to note any pertinent details.

'I've had the results back regarding the blue fibres found in the mouths of both victims,' Henry began, his excitement palpable even through the phone line. 'It's quite fascinating, actually. We found traces of paint and some resist, which is a special type of adhesive used for painting on silk.'

Lauren's pen flew across the page as she wrote. 'Go on,' she prompted.

'Well, based on the composition and distribution of these substances, I believe that the victims were suffocated by a hand-painted silk cushion.'

Lauren's heart rate picked up as the pieces started to fall into place in her mind. 'This is excellent, Henry. Can you tell me more about this resist?'

'Certainly,' Henry replied, warming to his subject. 'Resist is a gutta-like substance used in silk painting to create boundaries for the dyes. It's applied to the silk before the paint and prevents the colours from bleeding into each other. It's quite a specialised product, typically used by artists or textile designers.'

Lauren's pulse quickened. Alfie Hackett studied textile design.

'Are you certain it was present in both victims?' Lauren pressed.

'Absolutely,' Henry confirmed. 'The chemical signature was unmistakable in both cases. It's not something you'd find in everyday household items.'

'This is excellent. Thanks, Henry. I don't suppose you can you tell whether the cushion was newly painted, by any chance?' Lauren wondered if she was clutching at straws but you never knew when forensics was concerned.

'No, that's not possible,' Henry replied, a note of apology in his tone. 'The degradation process of these substances doesn't allow for that level of precision. However, I can say with certainty that the paint and resist were fully dried at the time of use.'

Lauren nodded, even though Henry couldn't see her. 'Thanks, Henry. This is incredibly helpful.'

'Happy to be of assistance, Inspector,' Henry said. 'I'm off to have some breakfast now and I'll send over the full report later.'

'Much appreciated, Henry. I take it you're still short staffed if you're at work this early.'

'Tell me about it,' the pathologist grumbled. 'And by all accounts the situation isn't going to improve soon. Bring on retirement, that's all I can say.'

Lauren grimaced. 'I hope you're joking.'

'Yes,' Henry said with a sigh. 'Although I'd be lying if I said the thought didn't enter my head every now and again but—'

'But you love your job too much,' Lauren said, finishing the sentence for him.

'You know me too well. Anyway, good luck. Such a waste of young lives. I hope these findings help you catch the killer.'

'So do I, Henry. So do I.' Lauren hung up, her thoughts already racing ahead.

Alfie Hackett was most definitely a person of interest given his connection to the victims, his illegal loan sharking and the course he was taking. This new evidence could be the link they needed to tie him directly to the murders.

She could hear the main office coming to life, now the team was arriving for the day, so she left her desk and headed in there, making a beeline for Ellie's desk.

'Right, listen up, everyone,' Lauren said, her voice ringing out across the open-plan space. She stood tall, commanding attention as her team looked up from their desks. With the exception of Matt, whom she didn't expect to have arrived yet anyway, the team were all present. 'I've heard back from Henry the pathologist, and he believes the victims were suffocated with a hand-painted silk cushion.' She paused, letting that sink in for a moment before continuing, her eyes scanning the room to gauge reactions. Each team member appeared intrigued. 'Alfie Hackett's studying textile design at university. So let's see if we can link this back to him. Ellie, can you get onto that?'

Ellie nodded efficiently, her chair swivelling towards her computer. 'Sure. I'll take a look at the syllabus to see what they study on the course.' Her fingers flew over her keyboard as she pulled up the relevant information.

Lauren stood there for a few seconds watching Ellie work, her foot tapping silently against the floor. She fought the urge to pace and to ask the officer to hurry up, realising that Ellie was working as fast as she could, and there was no one else who could work at that speed.

'Yes, there are several modules on silk painting,' Ellie finally confirmed, glancing up from her screen, a hint of excitement in her voice. 'I can't say for certain yet whether Hackett has taken them, because I haven't accessed his academic records. I can get them if you wish.'

Lauren nodded decisively. 'No need to access his records yet. We'll get him in for further questioning.' She turned to Jenna. 'Please contact the police in Barnstaple and ask them to bring Hackett to Penzance as soon as possible.'

'Yes, ma'am,' Jenna, who was already reaching for her phone, replied.

Lauren's gaze swept across the room again. 'Ellie, did you discover whether Finley Glenister had been borrowing money from other sources? I'm concerned that he might have borrowed from someone really dodgy.'

'I couldn't find anything, ma'am,' Ellie said, shaking her head, a note of frustration in her voice. 'Obviously if he'd borrowed cash, hadn't banked it, and there was no agreement in place, it wouldn't be possible to track, so I can't say for certain. But I won't stop digging.'

'Good. Did you find anything useful on the victims' phones?'

'No, ma'am,' Ellie responded. 'The couple messaged each other several times most days and there were messages with friends, but no red flags.'

'Okay, thanks,' Lauren said. 'Someone needs to get in touch with the Red Lion pub in Barnstaple. Hackett's got a very weak alibi for the night of the murders. Find out if anyone there remembers him being present and if so, what time he arrived and left. It's over a three-hour drive from there to Porthcurno so if he was seen even close to the pub when they were murdered, we can eliminate him.'

'Leave that with me, ma'am,' Billy said, straightening in his chair.

Lauren's phone buzzed, and she saw there was a text from Matt.

Dad's had a good night, seems a bit stronger this morning. I'll be in shortly.

Quickly, she typed out a reply. *Great news. See you soon.*

After sending the message, Lauren strode purposefully to the whiteboard. She uncapped a red marker pen and added 'silk cushion' under the evidence column. She then drew a line connecting it to Alfie Hackett's name and profile. Stepping back, she assessed the web of lines and notes with a critical eye, her fingers drumming lightly against her thigh.

'Okay, let's keep going,' Lauren said, raising her voice above the noise of the team working. 'I want Alfie Hackett looked into in much greater detail, including his movements in the days leading up to the murders. Also, I want his finances investigated. He said he had an inheritance and that's what he used to lend the money, but that needs confirming. Don't forget to check CCTV to see if his car has been located anywhere in the Penzance area recently.'

'What about Dylan Fairclough, ma'am? Is he now out of the frame?' Billy asked.

'No one's excluded from our enquiries. We'll be leaving to interview him shortly, while waiting for Alfie Hackett to arrive.'

SEVENTEEN
WEDNESDAY 13 SEPTEMBER

Matt had only been in the office for a few minutes before Lauren told him they were heading to Dylan Fairclough's house.

When they arrived, Lauren rang the bell, and within seconds, the door swung open, revealing a tall woman who looked to be in her late fifties. Her dark hair was styled in a short bob and her make-up flawless. Was she on her way out?

'Yes?' she answered, her voice polite but guarded.

'Mrs Fairclough?' Lauren asked, holding out her warrant card for the woman to see.

'Yes, that's me.'

'I'm DI Pengelly from Penzance police, and this is DS Price. Is Dylan in?'

'Is this about Finley and Jasmine?' Mrs Fairclough asked, her voice sounding concerned.

'Yes, we'd like to ask him a few more questions,' Lauren replied, her tone gentle but firm.

'I'm sorry, he's not here. He's at work. I tried to persuade him not to go in today, but he needs the money and can't afford to take any time off.'

'I see,' Lauren replied.

Matt raised an eyebrow, glancing around the well-appointed house. Surely they'd give him some money if he needed it.

Mrs Fairclough bristled slightly and her posture stiffened, as if being able to read Matt's mind. 'We do help him, from time to time. But my husband, Dylan's stepfather, is insistent that while he's at university, during the holidays he should be working. Dylan also pays board when he's living at home. It's good to teach your children real-life skills.'

'Yes, of course. I understand,' Matt said, nodding.

'Dylan also uses the name Fairclough,' Lauren commented.

'Yes, we married when Dylan was six and he took my husband's surname,' Mrs Fairclough replied.

Yet she still referred to him as the *stepfather*. Interesting.

'Dylan told us he worked at a bakery. Which one?' Lauren asked.

'The one in Albert Street. He finishes at six,' Mrs Fairclough said, her tone becoming more business-like.

'Thank you. While we're here, would you mind if we took a look around his bedroom?' Lauren asked, keeping her voice light.

Matt tensed slightly. This could be a crucial moment in their investigation.

'For what?' Mrs Fairclough asked, frowning.

'To see if there's anything that might assist with our enquiries. Something that he might not have thought was important when we last met with him,' Lauren explained.

Mrs Fairclough hesitated for a moment. 'Surely you don't think he's involved in what happened to Finley and Jasmine?'

'No – that's not why we're here,' Lauren assured her. 'We're talking to the couple's friends to get a fuller picture of their lives. Time's precious on this case, as I'm sure you appreciate, and that's why we'd rather look now than wait until he's home or apply for a search warrant.'

Mrs Fairclough's eyes widened at Lauren's words. 'Oh... of course you can check in there. I couldn't believe it when I heard about those poor kids. First, we were told suicide and now it's murder. Was it random? Were they unlucky being in the wrong place?'

'We don't know, until we receive the pathologist's report,' Lauren said. 'How well did you know the couple?'

'Finley, very well. He was like a permanent fixture here when they were at school. The boys were inseparable.' She shook her head and gave an unhappy sigh.

'How's Dylan coping?'

'He's devastated by Finley's death. We're all in shock, obviously. But he's taking it even worse than I would have imagined. It's dreadful.'

'What about Jasmine? How did that affect him?' Matt asked.

'Of course, he's upset about her, too, but in a different way,' Mrs Fairclough said, almost dismissively, which struck Matt as odd. 'Dylan didn't have the same history with Jasmine. They all went to school together, but Finley didn't start going out with Jasmine until they were in their final year. She came around here sometimes with Finley and they'd all sit upstairs in Dylan's room. Gaming, or chatting. You know what kids are like. I didn't know her as well as Finley, obviously. But she seemed a very nice girl. Always polite and friendly. It's such a shame this has happened.'

Clearly she had no idea of her son's obsession with Jasmine. Unless she was trying to distract them. Maybe she did know about her son's fixation and didn't approve. Especially after what had happened with his teacher. Or worse... Did she suspect her son being involved in the deaths somehow? It was the slight hesitation and the way she'd emphasised Dylan's closeness to Finley rather than Jasmine that alerted him.

'Thank you. Could you show us to Dylan's room now please?' Lauren asked.

They followed Mrs Fairclough upstairs, stopping at the last room on the right-hand side. 'In here,' she said, opening the door.

Lauren peered inside before turning to Mrs Fairclough. 'We'll have a quick look alone if you don't mind.'

'Okay, I'll go back downstairs,' Mrs Fairclough said, hovering for a while before turning and walking away.

Once she was out of sight, Lauren pulled on some disposable gloves, and Matt did the same. The familiar snap of latex against his skin grounded him, reminding him of the gravity of their task.

'Right, we already know about his obsession with Jasmine from the letters he sent to her. Let's see if there's anything else in here relating to it,' Lauren said.

Lauren headed over to the wardrobe and Matt went to the tall chest of drawers, which had a television on top.

'It's very neat in here. I'm sure I wasn't so tidy as a twenty-one-year-old,' Matt remarked as he carefully searched through the drawers of clothing, all neatly folded.

'But not too surprising,' Lauren replied, her voice muffled from inside the wardrobe. 'I was always tidy at that age.'

Matt pulled open the third drawer, in which there were shorts. He felt around and underneath the clothes his fingers brushed against a small box. His heart rate quickened as he pulled it out and lifted the lid. Inside, he found a number of photos featuring Jasmine; one black and one blue scrunchie; a chunky silver bracelet with a T-bar clasp and a gold signet ring. The discovery sent a chill down his spine.

'Ma'am, have a look at this,' he said, showing her the contents of the box.

Lauren's eyes widened as she took in the photos and trinkets. 'She can't have known some of those photos had been taken. Did these other items belong to her, I wonder?'

Matt nodded slowly, his head churning with the implications. 'I bet they do.'

'Look here,' Lauren said, pointing to one of the photos. 'The side of this one has been cut off leaving only Fairclough next to Jasmine; I wonder if the missing image was of Finley?'

'Quite likely, I'd say. Yet more evidence of his unhealthy obsession with Jasmine. But does that mean he murdered her?'

'Before we start jumping to conclusions, we need to find out where he was over last weekend,' Lauren said.

'Maybe he met up with Jasmine and she told him categorically no. And that, added to him knowing Finley was going to officially propose... Well, it could have sent him over the edge, ma'am.'

'Maybe. But we still have Alfie Hackett to consider. We're going to keep an open mind.'

'Shall we take this box as evidence, ma'am?' Matt asked, holding it up.

'No, we'll leave it here for now because we don't want to alert him. Put it back where you found it. But first, take a photo of the box and all the contents.'

'Will do. Do you wish to discuss her son's obsession with Jasmine with Mrs Fairclough?'

'No. In case she alerts him. The same goes for what happened between him and his teacher.'

Matt pulled out his phone, took several photos and then carefully replaced the box and closed the drawer.

They left the bedroom after taking a final look around and, after bidding farewell to Mrs Fairclough, went back to the car.

'If I had to choose between Hackett and Fairclough as our prime suspect I'd choose the latter, ma'am. What do you think?'

Lauren sighed. 'I think we need to step back and be more

objective. The letters and box of trinkets are concerning, but they don't prove anything beyond an extremely unhealthy obsession. We need to interview Fairclough again and see where that takes us. But before that we have Hackett to deal with.'

EIGHTEEN

WEDNESDAY 13 SEPTEMBER

Matt and Lauren walked side by side to the interview room where Alfie Hackett was waiting, their steps in sync. The familiar tension that always preceded a crucial interview was building in Matt and as they approached the door, he took a deep breath.

They entered the room and Matt's eyes immediately locked onto Hackett. The suspect was sitting at the table, a dour expression on his face, and his arms were folded in front of him. The air of confidence he had when they'd met previously was gone and instead, he appeared wary and defensive. This hostility and defensiveness in Hackett's demeanour raised Matt's suspicions.

'Why am I here?' Hackett asked angrily.

'Because we need to question you further, Mr Hackett,' Lauren replied firmly.

'Ever heard of the phone? Or even asking me to come here? There was no need to arrest me like that in front of everyone. How do you think that made me look?' He glared at them.

'You haven't been arrested,' Lauren replied coolly.

'Well, it's almost the same thing. The police came round to my house and took me away. My mum was scared to death.'

'Sergeant Price, the recording, please,' Lauren said, appearing to Matt as if she was trying to keep her irritation at bay.

Matt nodded and did as she asked. 'Interview on Wednesday, 13 September. Those present: Detective Inspector Pengelly, Detective Sergeant Price and...' He looked expectantly at Hackett.

'Alfie Joshua Hackett,' the man stated, his icy stare directed at Matt.

'Mr Hackett, we want to ask you about silk painting,' Lauren began calmly. 'I understand you have studied it.'

Hackett's lips pressed into a thin line. 'Part of my course involves examining textiles and their uses. Why?'

'Have you done much silk painting?' Lauren probed.

He paused for a few seconds, his eyes darting between Matt and Lauren. 'Ummm... Not really. I only scraped a pass on that particular unit of my course.'

Hackett's fingers drummed nervously on the table. He was hiding something. But what?

'So to confirm, you don't do it as a regular activity?' Lauren probed.

'That's correct,' Hackett responded.

Matt's phone pinged and he discreetly peeped at the screen. It was a text from Ellie.

Hackett has exhibited painted silks.

His eyes narrowed and he stared at Hackett, trying to gauge his reaction to the discussion on silk painting. Hackett's face remained impassive, but a bead of sweat had formed on his forehead.

'Mr Hackett, I believe you're not being truthful. I've been informed that some of your painted silks have been exhibited,'

Matt said evenly, observing the man closely. 'Surely that means you're much better at it than you've led us to believe?'

Hackett's cheeks flushed. 'That was ages ago and part of an exhibition for college.'

'Your work couldn't have been as bad as you told us if it was exhibited. Why did you lie?' Matt asked, locking eyes with him.

'I don't know.' Hackett shrugged dismissively, but it didn't hide the tension in his shoulders.

Matt leant forward, not willing to let him off the hook that easily. 'Try again, Mr Hackett. Why did you lie?'

'Look... I had nothing to do with the deaths of Finley Glenister and his girlfriend, okay?' Hackett snapped defensively, his voice rising. 'I'm not stupid and it seems that silk painting has something to do with the murders, or you wouldn't be asking me about it. I didn't want to be implicated for something I didn't do so I downplayed my ability. That's all.'

'So you say,' Lauren said, her voice cool. 'Except now you've made it worse for yourself. What pieces of silk painting did you exhibit?'

Hackett sighed heavily, his shoulders sagging. 'Cushions.'

Yes. They were definitely onto something.

'I see. Where are these cushions?' Lauren enquired, her tone deceptively casual.

'They were sold.'

'When and where did you sell them? On the day they were exhibited? Afterwards? In a shop?' Lauren asked, her questions coming rapid-fire.

Hackett shifted in his seat. 'They were sold through the exhibition, I think. But I can't really remember. All I know is that I don't have them and haven't for a while.'

'I find it very hard to believe that you don't remember. Surely you have pride in your work?' Lauren asked, her foot tapping impatiently on the floor.

'The exhibition was about nine months ago,' Hackett

explained, haltingly, his eyes flitting around the room as if seeking an escape. 'I've produced lots of work since then, that's why I can't remember exactly.'

'What colour were your cushions?' Matt asked.

'They were designed using a blue colour palette,' Hackett replied, his voice low.

The same colour used in the murders.

Coincidence?

No way.

This wasn't looking good for Hackett.

'We need to locate the cushions you made,' Lauren declared, her tone brooking no argument.

'I don't know where they are,' Hackett protested, his voice rising again. 'Check with the university and see what happened to them after they were sold. They might be able to tell you who bought them.' He sucked in a loud breath. 'Look... silk cushions aren't unusual and can be bought in loads of gift shops. So I don't see why mine are important.'

'I don't know about this stuff, so tell me: when they have exhibitions, are pieces exhibited often sold?' Matt asked, trying to sound nonplussed despite the excitement building inside him.

'Yes, it's quite common,' Hackett confirmed, nodding vigorously.

Matt's phone pinged again. This time it was a message from Clem:

Hackett's car seen near Penzance on Saturday afternoon at three pm.

How was he going to get out of this one?

Matt nudged Lauren's foot to indicate that he was about to say something important, and sucked in a deep breath before confronting their suspect.

'Mr Hackett, I've been informed that you were actually in Penzance on Saturday.'

'No,' Hackett objected vehemently, his face reddening. 'I told you, I went to the pub.'

'Yes, you did, but your story about the pub was vague and we haven't yet been able to confirm it. Your car was seen on CCTV in Penzance during the afternoon. If it wasn't you driving then who was it?' Matt stared directly at the man.

Hackett's defiance visibly crumbled and his shoulders slumped. He lowered his gaze to the table. 'Okay. It was me.' Hackett bit down on his bottom lip nervously. 'I came over to meet Faith.'

'For a date?' Matt pressed, leaning forward slightly.

'I wasn't sure at the time but hoped it was,' Hackett replied, his shoulders sagging. 'Then, when we met it turned out to be all about Finley. She wanted me to stop pestering him for the money he owed because he was getting very upset and didn't have any money to pay me back. She asked me to give him more time.'

Something wasn't quite right. There had to be more to the story.

'You're telling us that you drove three hours to meet Faith in person, and all she did was ask you to stop bothering Finley about the money? That must have really pissed you off,' Matt said.

Hackett's fingers drummed a restless rhythm on the table. 'Maybe I was. But I wanted to see her and thought we could hang out together.'

'And did you?' Matt asked, leaning forward slightly.

'We were together for a while but then she left me to meet up with her friends.'

'I bet that made you really angry,' Lauren pushed, her voice sharp.

Hackett's nostrils flared and his posture stiffened. 'I drove for three hours so what do you think?'

'Did you stay in Penzance after Faith left you? Maybe go for a drive to Porthcurno Beach?' Lauren asked.

'I did drive around for a while but I can't remember where. Then I went home and met my friends in the pub at night like I told you. I was back in Barnstaple by eight. And that's the truth.'

'Right, well, we'll be speaking to Faith about this,' Lauren said firmly. 'For now, you'll be kept in custody overnight.'

'What? I've told you everything I know. I didn't have anything to do with the deaths, I swear.' Hackett's voice rose in desperation, his eyes wide with panic.

'You were in Penzance on Saturday and you lied to us about it,' Lauren pointed out sternly.

'Only because I didn't want to get involved,' Hackett pleaded, his composure completely shattered.

Matt shook his head. 'It doesn't work that way, I'm afraid. You're already involved.'

They left Hackett in the interview room, the suspect's protests fading as the door closed behind them. They'd made progress, but there were still so many unanswered questions.

'What do we do now, ma'am?' Matt asked.

'Tomorrow Jasmine's friend is coming in for an interview and after that, we'll visit Faith to get confirmation of Hackett's story.' She paused. 'We need someone to contact local gift shops to see if silk-painted cushions are as readily available as Hackett claims. Also, ask someone to find out whether the university has a record of who bought the cushions he exhibited. We'll leave Hackett in a cell overnight. It might encourage him to open up.'

'And Dylan Fairclough? Where does that leave him?' Matt asked.

'He's still a person of interest. But we'll speak to him tomorrow also. He has no idea that we're aware of his obsession with Jasmine which goes in our favour and means he's hardly likely to do a runner, or anything stupid like that.'

NINETEEN

THURSDAY 14 SEPTEMBER

Matt arrived at work around nine, and the moment he'd walked through the door he was greeted by smiles from the team members.

'Hey, Sarge, how's your dad?' Billy asked. The young officer's face was lined with genuine concern.

'Much better, thanks, Billy,' Matt replied.

'I thought you looked brighter,' Billy said warmly.

'I visited him last night and he seemed almost back to his old self, but he's going to be on medication for good now. Thanks for asking.' It was moments like these that reminded Matt why he loved working with this team. They truly cared about each other.

'That's great,' Billy replied.

Glancing over to Lauren's office, he couldn't see her silhouette. 'Where's the DI?' he asked, nodding towards her room.

'She's gone to see the DCI about the case. They're holding a press conference later today,' Jenna informed him, looking up from her screen, which she'd been studying intently.

'Thanks. Do you have a time for Ruby Bennington's

arrival?' Matt asked, remembering that Jasmine's friend was due in to see them.

'She's on her way. We're expecting her before ten,' Jenna replied, checking her watch.

'Excellent. Has anyone looked into gift shops selling silk-printed cushions?'

'Yes, me,' Clem said, swivelling in his chair to face Matt. 'Hackett was right. They're readily available all over Cornwall. I've contacted several shops in the area to see if anyone recalled selling any that were mainly blue, but none of them could remember the exact details of the cushions on sale. I've asked them all to check their credit and debit card transactions just in case they find something.'

Matt furrowed his brow, processing the information. 'So, when we say, "readily available", what does that mean exactly? That they're everywhere and it would be impossible to track them?'

'A lot of places do sell them,' Clem clarified, shrugging apologetically.

'Okay, that's not very helpful,' Matt sighed.

'I've checked with the university, Sarge, regarding their exhibitions,' Jenna added. 'All exhibits are up for sale but the university doesn't keep a detailed record of sales because a lot of people pay cash. I've also asked them to check any card receipts but to be honest it seems like we have another dead end, I'm afraid.'

Matt was about to respond when Lauren appeared. Her face was set in its usual determined expression, but it didn't hide the slight shadows under her eyes that spoke of long hours and sleepless nights.

'Matt, if you've got a moment, please,' she said, beckoning for him to come over.

He headed over to where she was standing. 'Yes, ma'am?'

'I've been with the DCI. There's going to be a press conference this afternoon, which fortunately I'm not needed for. The DCI will ask for people who saw anything Saturday evening or early Sunday morning to come forward. There might have been someone on the beach who witnessed the couple being there.'

'That's great, ma'am,' Matt replied. Sometimes, all it took was one witness to break a case wide open. 'Will you be announcing that the deaths are suspicious?'

'He won't explicitly state the cause of deaths although no doubt someone from the media will ask. He's planning to fob them off by saying that we're still waiting for the pathologist's report.'

'Unless a family member or friend leaks the details,' Matt said with a grimace.

'If they do, we'll have to deal with it. It's not going to impinge on the investigation either way.' Lauren's expression softened slightly. 'How's your dad?'

'He's doing fine,' Matt replied before continuing. 'We've got Ruby Bennington coming in shortly, and after that we'll visit Faith Glenister to discuss her meeting with Alfie Hackett. Then we'll catch up with Dylan Fairclough. Is that still the plan for today?'

'Yes,' Lauren confirmed.

'What about Alfie Hackett?'

'We'll speak to him later. He's fine staying where he is. Let me know when Ruby Bennington arrives.'

Matt nodded and was about to head back to his desk when he spotted Jenna hurrying towards them.

'Ruby Bennington's here already,' the officer said when she reached them.

'Great. Thanks, Jenna. Come on, Matt,' Lauren said, with a smile.

When they entered the interview room, Ruby Bennington stared up at them. She was a petite woman with a short blonde pixie haircut and looked younger than her twenty-one years. She gripped the arms of her chair.

'Good morning, Ruby. Thank you for coming in to see us,' Lauren said warmly in a tone that Matt hoped would put the young woman at ease and get her talking. 'I'm sorry that we had to interrupt your holiday by giving you such devastating news about Jasmine and Finley.'

'I'm glad to have heard it from you, because otherwise I might have seen it online and that would have been even worse. I'm sorry I couldn't get here sooner but the flights and everything...' Ruby's voice trailed off and she fidgeted nervously, her eyes darting around the room.

'That's totally fine. I'm very sorry for your loss.' Lauren paused for a few seconds so the young woman could collect herself. 'We understand from Jasmine's parents that the two of you were best friends?' Lauren continued, her tone soothing.

'Yes, we have been for years. We went to school together and then applied to the same university.'

'Several of your friends from school went to Southampton University. Was that planned?' Lauren asked.

'Sort of. We wanted to stay together and it is a top uni.' She leant forward slightly, counting on her fingers. 'There was me, Jasmine, Finley, Dylan, and Faith started a year later. But we all applied for different courses.'

'What are you studying?' Lauren asked, tilting her head slightly.

'French and maths,' Ruby replied, her eyes lighting up.

'That's an unusual combination,' Lauren remarked, raising an eyebrow.

Ruby nodded, a small smile tugging at the corners of her mouth. 'People often say that but actually it's very common.'

'Do you go to France as part of the course?' Lauren asked, shifting slightly in her seat.

'In my third year, I get to spend twelve months there.

Jasmine was going to come over for some of the holidays to visit me but—' Ruby's eyes glazed over, glistening with unshed tears, which she brushed away with her hand. 'Sorry. It's been so hard ever since I found out what had happened.'

'It's okay. We understand. Would you like a break? I can get you some water,' Lauren offered.

'No, I'm fine to carry on, thank you,' Ruby said with a sniff.

'Did you go to Australia and New Zealand with Jasmine, Finley and Faith during their gap year?' Lauren asked.

'No because I had a job in France teaching English as a foreign language. I wish I had gone, though, because they had such a great time,' Ruby said with a sigh.

'Did you share a flat with Jasmine and Finley?' Lauren asked.

'No, I share with several girls on my course.'

Lauren frowned. 'How come you didn't want to live with them if you're such good friends?'

'I would have shared with Jasmine, in an all-girls flat, but I said no because it was mixed. It's easier living with girls. Boys tend to be messy in their student flats. Well, not all boys obviously but a lot of them are. I don't know if you ever remember?' Ruby gave a tiny laugh and then, as if remembering about the deaths of her friends, she halted and sucked in a steadying breath.

'I do indeed,' Lauren said with a wry smile.

Matt didn't enter the conversation, as he didn't go to university. He went straight into the police force at eighteen after he'd completed his A levels. But he continued observing Ruby closely, looking for any signs of deception or hidden knowledge. There wasn't any. She appeared to be telling the truth. Although he knew from experience that appearances could be deceptive.

'What can you tell us about Jasmine and Finley's relationship?' Matt asked, leaning forward slightly.

Tears formed in Ruby's eyes and she blinked them away. 'It was good. Ever since they started going out when she was seventeen, it was only ever him for Jasmine. She never even looked at another guy.' Ruby exhaled loudly. 'Everyone loved Jasmine. You'd never hear anyone bitching about her. She was always upbeat. I can't understand why they'd kill themselves. It makes no sense.' She scrunched up her eyes and lowered her head.

The young woman needed to know the truth before someone else told her. It was up to them to deliver the news.

'I'm sorry to have to tell you this, Ruby, but they didn't take their own lives,' Lauren said gently.

'What?' she said, looking up at them, her eyes wide. 'Was it an accident?'

'No. We're treating their deaths as suspicious.'

'Oh my goodness... You mean they were *murdered*.' Ruby collapsed back in the chair. 'I don't believe it.'

'Can you think of anyone who might bear a grudge against them, or even just one of them?' Lauren asked.

'This makes no sense at all. I don't know anyone who hated them enough to kill them,' Ruby said, shaking her head vehemently.

'What can you tell us about Finley's gambling?' Matt asked, deciding to move the interview on.

Ruby's mouth dropped open. 'You think it could be because of that?'

'We don't know for certain but it is an avenue we're pursuing,' Matt said, leaning in towards her.

'You know, at one time, Jasmine was really worried about it. She lent him money when she could, but she didn't have much. Her parents aren't rich, like Finley's. Jas didn't tell me it had got that bad, though. I thought he was trying to stop.' Ruby held the silver chain around her neck in her hand and twisted it around her fingers.

'Do you know Alfie Hackett from university?' Lauren asked.

'Umm, no... I don't think so.'

'He lent Finley money.'

'I might know his face but the name doesn't register. Jasmine didn't tell me that Finley had borrowed money from someone. Unless she didn't know. Finley might not have told her. It wouldn't surprise me.'

'Why do you say that?' Matt asked, quirking an eyebrow.

'He knew how strongly Jasmine felt about his gambling so he might have kept it a secret to stop her from worrying. He could be secretive when he wanted to be and—' She covered her mouth with her hand. 'Sorry, I shouldn't speak badly about him. Not now he's... he's dead.'

'You're not,' Matt said. 'You're helping us discover what happened to them.'

'To clarify, you think that Jasmine wouldn't have known that Finley owed money to Hackett?' Lauren asked.

Ruby turned her attention to the DI. 'Well, if she did, she didn't say anything to me and we tell each other everything. So on that basis I'd say she didn't know.' Ruby exhaled loudly. 'I can't believe that they were murdered.' Her voice caught on the last word.

'We're so sorry.' Lauren paused. 'I know this must be a huge shock for you. Would you like a few minutes' break before we continue?'

Ruby shook her head, as tears slightly fell down her cheeks. 'No, I can carry on. Have you spoken to Dylan Fairclough, Finley's so-called best friend?' The young woman's face hardened slightly.

'Why did you say *so-called*?' Matt asked, leaning in.

Ruby paused, her eyes darting between Matt and Lauren. 'Dylan's not who you think he is. He says he's Finley's best friend, but he had a massive thing for Jasmine. He wanted to split them up and go out with her. He tried a few times but it didn't work.'

'How do you know?' Lauren asked, frowning.

'Because Jasmine told me. He sent her letters declaring his love.'

'Did you see them?'

'Yes. She was going to throw them away in case Finley found them, but I persuaded her to keep them.'

'Why?'

Ruby exhaled loudly. 'I don't know. You'll probably think I was being stupid, but they seemed a bit over the top. Like he was overly fixated with her. So it was in case it blew up into something... it was just a feeling I had.'

'Did you think the letters could be evidence?' Matt prompted, sensing Lauren's eyes on him. Was she annoyed that he'd spelt it in that way rather than waiting for Ruby to say that?

'Maybe... I'm not sure.'

'What did Jasmine think of Dylan?' Matt asked, his voice carefully controlled.

'She liked him but not in that way and she made it clear that they could never be together because she was with Finley. Jasmine thought that he'd accepted her decision but...' Her voice faded away.

'Did Jasmine consider telling Finley about Dylan's obsession with her?' Lauren asked.

'We talked about whether she should mention it but, in the end, she decided not to because she didn't want to cause any friction between Fin and Dylan and ruin their friendship. That was what she was like. Always thinking of others,' Ruby said, a sob escaping her throat.

'Did you know that Finley and Jasmine were going to get engaged?' Lauren asked.

'They'd been talking about it for a long time but hadn't got around to it.'

'When they were found on the beach, there was an empty ring box beside them, and a ring on her finger.'

Ruby's eyebrows shot up. 'Oh, she didn't tell me. But then of course... why would she? I was on holiday and we had very limited Wi-Fi.' A brief flash of hurt crossed her face.

'Finley bought the engagement ring last week and Dylan went with him to choose it.'

Matt could almost see the wheels turning in Ruby's head as she processed this new information. Her eyes narrowed, and she leant forward, her voice barely above a whisper.

'Do you think that was the last straw for Dylan? Was he responsible for their...'

She was a bright girl, seeming to piece things together in the same way they were.

'No, no, that's not what we're saying,' Lauren said. 'Although now you've mentioned it, do you think that it's possible?'

'No. Surely not...' Ruby muttered.

'Does Dylan have a temper?' Matt asked pointedly.

'He can get wound up about things which maybe other people wouldn't,' Ruby said.

Was she trying to be tactful? And why?

'Can you give us an example?' Matt asked.

'Well, one time another guy asked Jasmine out and she told the gang, and Dylan went and sorted it out. He said he'd done it for Finley. But Finley had just laughed it off.'

'What do you mean by *sorted it out*?' Matt asked.

'I didn't see it myself, but the guy did have a black eye and a broken nose.'

Matt shared a meaningful look with Lauren. The evidence was mounting against Dylan Fairclough. His obsession with Jasmine, his temper and his possessiveness. The pieces were falling into place, but they needed hard evidence to make anything stick.

'Is there anything else you can think of that might help?' Lauren asked.

'No... I hope... I'm so stunned that somebody killed them. I don't know how it could be anything to do with Jasmine. But I don't know...' Ruby appeared totally drained.

It was time to end the interview.

'Well, thank you very much for coming in,' Lauren said. 'If you do think of anything, here's my card.'

Ruby took it and held it tightly in her hand.

Matt and Lauren escorted Ruby to the station entrance and watched as she left the building. Her grief was evident in every step she took.

'Poor kid,' he said as he turned back to Lauren. 'Learning your best friend was murdered.'

'I felt bad about breaking it to her like that but what else could I do?' Lauren bowed her head slightly.

'It couldn't be avoided,' Matt said, wanting to ease his boss's guilty feelings. 'When we speak to Faith about Hackett, we should mention Fairclough and get her take on him and his infatuation with Jasmine. If she knows about it, that is.'

Lauren nodded in agreement as they headed back to the station car park.

The case was getting more twisted with each new piece of information. Everything was now pointing towards Fairclough, but experience had taught Matt that things were rarely as straightforward as they seemed.

Lauren pulled up outside the large home belonging to the Glenisters, the gravel crunching under the car's tyres. Despite the grandness of the house, today it seemed to carry an air of sadness, as if the building itself was mourning the loss of Finley.

With Matt at her side, she made her way to the front door, her footsteps echoing in the quiet morning air. She took a moment to straighten her jacket and collect her thoughts before ringing the bell, knowing that once again she'd be intruding on their grief.

The chime echoed inside the house, followed by slow, heavy footsteps.

Mr Glenister answered. Grief was etched into every feature.

'Good morning, Detective Inspector,' he said, his voice low and hardly audible.

'Hello, Mr Glenister. We'd like to speak to you all if we may. Including Faith if she's here.'

'Oh yes, she's home. We've been discussing going shopping for food. We haven't actually left the house since Sunday.

Neighbours have been very good, coming round with meals, but I suppose we need to start getting back to normal life, if we can.' He gave a resigned sigh.

Lauren nodded sympathetically. 'I understand, but these things take time and it's best to go at your own pace.'

'Please, come through,' Mr Glenister said, barely acknowledging Lauren's comment. They walked into the house and followed him into the snug. 'I'll fetch my wife and daughter.'

Lauren took in the family photos on the walls. One in particular caught her attention: a candid shot of Finley and Faith when they were very young. Their arms were wrapped around each other, faces frozen in mid-laughter. The camera had captured a moment of pure, unguarded joy between the siblings, a stark contrast to the sombre atmosphere now permeating the house.

After a few minutes, the three of them walked in and sat opposite Lauren and Matt. Mrs Glenister was like a zombie, acting like she was on autopilot. Lauren's heart went out to her. Losing a child was every parent's worst nightmare. Mr Glenister's arm hovered protectively near his wife, as if afraid she might crumble at any moment.

'Is Sonia here?' Lauren asked, referring to the family liaison officer who'd been allocated to them.

'She was, but had to go somewhere. She said she'd only be gone an hour. We didn't mind,' Mr Glenister said. 'She's been very good.'

'I'm glad,' Lauren said, wondering what was so important that the FLO had to leave them. She'd follow up on that later. 'Sonia mentioned to you our discovery that Finley owed quite a lot of money, which we believe he might have borrowed for gambling. She reported back that you were unaware of this debt.'

Mr Glenister flushed slightly and his hands clenched into fists. 'In the past I've given him money to pay his debts, but more recently I refused. I told him he had to deal with it himself like an adult. He assured me that he had. But it appears he lied to me. This debt... it's not the reason...' His voice trailed off, regret shining from his eyes.

Lauren traded a look with Matt. 'We don't know yet, but we do have someone in custody. The man who lent him money.'

'Alfie Hackett?' Faith exclaimed.

'Yes, that's correct,' Matt confirmed. 'You knew that your brother borrowed from him, didn't you?'

'Yes. I saw them in the student union bar having a heated discussion and asked Fin what it was about. He wouldn't tell me initially, but I got it out of him.' Faith glanced at her parents, and bit down on her bottom lip. 'I know I should have told you, but Finley made me promise not to.' She returned her gaze to Lauren. 'Surely you don't believe that Alfie had anything to do with their deaths.'

'We're not discounting anyone,' Lauren explained, keeping her tone neutral and not wanting to give anything away.

Mr Glenister's face paled. 'Why didn't he come to me?'

'Because you told him not to, Dad, and he didn't want to upset you,' Faith said, a tiny sigh escaping her lips.

Lauren cleared her throat. 'I'm sorry for the pain this is causing. Before we go, we'd like a quick word with Faith alone, please.'

Mrs Glenister's head snapped up, suddenly animated. 'Why can't we stay with her?' she demanded.

Before Lauren could respond, Faith cut in. 'I'll be fine, Mum. Don't worry.'

'Yes, I know,' her mother persisted, reaching out to touch her daughter's arm. 'But you might want someone with you.'

'There's nothing to worry about, Mrs Glenister. We have some routine questions for Faith, that's all,' Lauren reassured kindly, trying to defuse the tension.

'Okay,' Mrs Glenister said reluctantly as she left the room with her husband.

Lauren turned her attention back to Faith. She seemed to be holding up well, given the circumstances. But Lauren knew from experience that there were many ways people dealt with the death of a loved one. Some fell apart, others put on a brave face. Some were constantly angry. Which category did this young woman fall into?

'Thanks, Faith,' Lauren said. 'We want to ask you more about Alfie Hackett. He claims to have visited Penzance on Saturday to meet up with you. Is that correct?'

'Yes. I asked him to.' Faith's voice was steady, but she was fidgeting with the hem of her shirt.

'That's why we didn't want to speak in front of your parents, in case you didn't want them to know,' Lauren said, lowering her voice.

'Thanks. They've got enough to worry about as it is. It's so hard for them and I'm not sure what I can do to help.' Her eyes filled with tears and she swept them away with the back of her hand.

'These are difficult times for all of you. Everyone deals with their grief in a different way. All you can do is be there for them,' Lauren said, hoping to pacify her. 'And they'll be here for you, too.'

'Yes, I know.' Faith's shoulders slumped, as if it was all getting too much for her.

'Returning to Alfie, why did you ask to see him?' Lauren asked.

'To stop him from threatening Finley? I mean, there was no point. Finley would get him the money when he could. But Alfie suddenly turned funny about it.' Faith shook her head. 'I thought it would help.'

'Did Finley know that you were going to ask Alfie to back off?' Matt asked.

'No. I didn't tell him in case he told me not to. You know, when I met up with Alfie, he told me that if I agreed to go out with him on a date, he'd stop pestering Finley for the money.' She gave a shallow laugh. 'Can you believe that.'

Lauren sat up straighter, intrigued by the revelation. 'He did? Were you surprised?' Her fingers drummed lightly on the arm rest.

'After the initial shock and I thought about it, I suppose not. I've always been friendly towards him but at the back of my mind wondered if there was a bit more on his side. Not that I encouraged him, because I didn't. But sometimes I'd catch him staring at me.' Faith's shoulders tensed slightly as she spoke.

'What answer did you give to his suggestion?' Matt asked.

'I told him it wasn't a good idea and we should stay as friends.' Faith's gaze flicked briefly to one side.

'Not even to stop him from going after Finley for the money?' Matt asked, his eyebrow lifted.

'That would be deceitful and unfair to everyone. I thought I'd be able to persuade him anyway,' Faith said with a gentle shrug, her hands splaying open.

'Then what happened?' Lauren asked, leaning back in her chair.

'He seemed okay about it and agreed to give Finley a bit more time to pay.' Faith's fingers traced patterns on the sofa cushion. 'But I didn't get the chance to tell my brother because...' Her voice broke. 'Sorry,' she said, sniffing.

'Did you offer Finley any money to pay off his debts?' Matt asked.

'I didn't have any, so no. I pay my own way at university, and if there's any money left over it goes on buying art supplies. I draw in my spare time.' Faith brightened slightly at the mention of her hobby. 'Something totally different from quantum physics.'

'I was never any good at science at school,' Lauren said,

tucking a stray hair behind her ear as she spoke. 'You didn't fancy doing art then?'

Faith appeared confused by the sudden shift in topic and her lips pursed thoughtfully as she answered. 'I'd have loved to, but my teachers wanted me to study something more academic. I'm happy to draw in my spare time. And I do love science... although I've been thinking about dropping out for a year. I don't know if I can face going back yet and Mum and Dad will need me here.' Tears began to run down her cheek. 'Do you know when we can have the funeral?' she suddenly asked.

'Sorry, I don't have that information yet. The funeral can't take place while the investigation's ongoing and the pathologists are still working. I know this is difficult, but it's a necessary part of the process,' Lauren responded, the sound of the raw pain in Faith's voice suddenly getting to her.

'Oh,' Faith said quietly, her body seeming to collapse in on itself.

Lauren could see the young woman was struggling, but she still had avenues to pursue. In hindsight, perhaps it would have been prudent to allow the parents to stay during the questioning.

'We won't keep you for much longer, Faith, but I do have something to ask. When we interviewed Ruby Bennington, Jasmine's best friend, she mentioned that Dylan Fairclough was infatuated with Jasmine in a way that was less than healthy. It's been going on for several years, since they were at school. We've also discovered some evidence which we believe validates her claims. Were you aware of this?'

'What? Are you sure?' Faith said, her eyes widened in surprise. But a fleeting twitch at the corner of her mouth alerted Lauren she might not have been as shocked as she was making out.

'Apparently he tried to split up Finley and Jasmine because he wanted to go out with her himself,' Lauren explained.

Faith shook her head vehemently, her fingers briefly curling into her palms. 'No, that can't be right. I'd have known. Someone would have said something. Or I'd have noticed. And you say it began in school? If that's right wouldn't Jasmine have told me? I know Ruby was her best friend but on our gap year we got closer... are you sure? I don't even remember her mentioning Dylan's name when we were overseas.'

Faith stared into the distance, as if she was mentally going through the previous years, searching for anything that would confirm what she'd been told.

'You don't believe this, then?' Lauren asked, after a while.

Faith took a few seconds before meeting Lauren's eyes again. 'I'm not saying it isn't true, because I don't really know. And you said there's evidence. But I can't get my head around it.' She paused, her shoulders tensing almost imperceptibly as her gaze flicked from Lauren to Matt and back again. 'Does that mean you think Dylan murdered my brother and Jasmine?'

'We are investigating all possibilities,' Lauren said calmly.

'I thought you believed it to be Alfie Hackett.'

'Like I said, we're still investigating,' Lauren repeated.

'But you haven't eliminated him.' Faith locked eyes with Lauren as if trying to see what was going on in her head.

'No, not yet. But that doesn't mean—'

'No way would Dylan have anything to do with their deaths. He's been our friend for years. Even if he did love Jasmine he wouldn't have gone that far. You've got it wrong,' Faith interrupted. She ran a hand through her hair, confusion etched across her face. 'But... I don't know. Maybe it is true...' She exhaled loudly. 'No, it can't be... I don't know what to think. This is so confusing.'

'Do you believe Alfie Hackett to be capable?' Lauren pressed, returning to the man they currently had in custody.

Faith paused, considering. 'I don't know. I would have said no, but honestly, I'm sorry, I... I can't tell you. This is too much to wrap my head around.' She leant forward, her head buried in her hands.

Lauren reached out and placed a comforting hand on Faith's arm. 'I'm sorry, I know this is hard for you. But you've been very helpful. Thank you.'

As they stood to leave, Lauren's thoughts whirled. Alfie's obsession with Faith; Dylan's alleged infatuation with Jasmine. There were potential motives and complex relationships to untangle. But which one had led to the murders?

'We're going to see ourselves out. We'll say goodbye to your parents as we go,' Lauren said.

Faith nodded mutely, seemingly lost in her own thoughts. Lauren couldn't blame her. Her world had been shattered.

Once they'd left the property, Lauren turned to Matt. 'Well, Hackett or Fairclough?'

Matt shrugged. 'Could be either. Or both. Or neither. We need to keep digging, although I'm leaning towards Fairclough.'

'Agreed. Let's get back to the station and see what else we can turn up.'

'Yes, ma'am.'

In the car, Lauren sat for a moment before starting the engine. 'Matt, did you notice how Faith reacted when we mentioned Dylan's supposed feelings for Jasmine? She tried to hide it with a shocked expression and words... But it seemed a bit forced.'

Matt nodded. 'Yes, I did see that. And the thought that she really wasn't surprised did cross my mind. But why hide it, now. Why not tell us the truth?'

'That's what we need to find out. We'll dig deeper into the dynamics of this friendship group. There's more going on here than meets the eye. When we get back, I want to review all interviews so far. There's got to be something we've missed.'

Matt nodded in agreement. 'I'll get the team to compile everything we have. Maybe a fresh look will reveal something new.'

TWENTY-ONE
THURSDAY 14 SEPTEMBER

'Okay, everyone,' Lauren said, as the team fell into silence ready for the update. Matt followed close behind, mirroring her own determination. 'Ruby Bennington has confirmed what we already know about Dylan Fairclough's obsession with Jasmine Dodd. We also know that Alfie Hackett has a thing for Faith Glenister and agreed to wait a while for repayment of the loan if she'd go out with him. She refused but he still agreed to wait for his money.'

'Does that mean we let Hackett go, ma'am?' Billy asked.

'We can't discount him as a suspect yet. He had a motive, too. Finley owed him money, and Faith rejected him. That's a double blow to his ego. We also need his alibi confirming. Who's working on that?'

'Me, ma'am,' Clem said. 'But I haven't been able to get hold of anyone at the pub yet. I'll keep trying.'

'Thanks. We need to investigate Dylan Fairclough further. He wanted Jasmine for himself and that gives him a clear motive if he thought it wasn't going to happen.' She wrote Fairclough's name on the board with a dotted arrow connecting him to Jasmine and a full line connecting him to Finley because they were best friends. 'But the question is, did he act on it? And, if so, in what way?'

Matt stepped forward, his arms crossed over his chest. 'I think we should look at the timeline, ma'am. When exactly did Fairclough's obsession with Jasmine begin? Was it before or after she got together with Finley? And what were his true feelings when they got engaged? We know he was with Finley when they bought the ring and he told us he was happy about it, but all this suggests he most likely wasn't.'

Lauren nodded, her eyes narrowing as she considered the possibilities. 'If Fairclough's feelings for Jasmine started before she got together with Finley, then it's possible he saw his friend as an obstacle, someone standing in the way of what he wanted. But if his obsession developed later, after they were already a couple, then maybe the engagement was the trigger. That could be the moment he realised he'd lost her for good.' She began to sketch out a rough timeline on the board, the squeak of the marker punctuating her words. The familiar act of visualising the case helped to organise her thoughts. 'We also have to remember that he has a tendency towards obsessive behaviour, as confirmed by what happened when he was at school with his teacher. I want you all to continue researching into him while I go with Sergeant Price to interview him again. By the way, what's happening regarding the house-to-house on Porthcurno Beach?'

'I spoke to the officers who went out there but nobody they questioned had anything to tell them – and there weren't even any door cams to check footage,' Clem said.

Matt raised an eyebrow. 'There are no cameras? Seriously? I know many people don't have them in Cornwall, but surely in such a touristy area with so many strangers hanging around someone must have one. Are you sure the officers actually looked and didn't just say they had when you asked?'

'Sorry, I can't answer that, Sarge. I can hardly challenge them on it, can I?' Clem answered, sounding slightly defensive.

'No, of course not,' Matt said, giving a dismissive wave of his hand.

Lauren glanced at her sergeant. It wasn't like him to accuse fellow officers like that.

'We should check anyway,' Lauren said. A tension headache was beginning to form at her temples and she gave them a rub. 'We'll go out ourselves and not rely on the PCs.'

'Are you sure, ma'am?' Clem asked, hesitation in his voice. 'Isn't that going to be a waste of time, going over the same thing more than once?'

Lauren understood his concern, but she couldn't shake the feeling that they were missing something. 'I still think it's worth following up. Just in case.'

'I'll go, ma'am,' Jenna said eagerly.

'Me, too,' Billy added, already reaching for his black leather bomber jacket, which he'd hung on the back of his chair.

'Concentrate on the houses closest to the beach. Talk to everyone to see if anyone remembers seeing Jasmine and Finley that day. Even the smallest detail could be important.' Lauren turned to Clem. 'I want you to check the CCTV footage again with particular reference to Fairclough's car. Go wider than Porthcurno itself and find out if he was in the vicinity on Saturday evening or Sunday morning.'

Clem nodded, pulling his keyboard towards him. 'On it, ma'am.'

Lauren sighed, rubbing her temples again as the headache intensified. She checked the clock on the wall. The day was slipping away, and they still had so much ground to cover.

'I want to be kept up to date on anything found,' Lauren said to the team. She then turned to Matt. 'Okay, let's get moving. We'll go to the bakery first to check if Fairclough's at work.'

'How are we going to play the interview, ma'am? Are we going to tell him what we found in his bedroom?' Matt asked.

'I'm not sure. If we go in too hard then he's likely to clam up. We need to lead him gently.'

As they went to leave, a wave of exhaustion swept over Lauren. The case was already taking its toll, both physically and emotionally.

'Are you okay?' Matt asked as they headed out of the station and into the bright sunlight.'

'Yes, why?' Lauren asked, turning to him with a frown.

'You keep grimacing.'

'I've got a headache, that's all,' Lauren said, running her fingers across her forehead. 'It's nothing I can't deal with once I've taken a couple of paracetamols. Now, come on, let's hope that Dylan Fairclough can give us something.'

Matt nodded. 'Agreed. But we do need to keep an open mind. Dylan Fairclough's obsession with Jasmine could give him a motive, but he might not be the only one to want the couple dead.'

TWENTY-TWO
THURSDAY 14 SEPTEMBER

Lauren pushed open the door to the bakery, a quaint shop with a large window full of cakes and pastries that seemed at odds with the unpleasant purpose she and Matt were there for. The scent of fresh baking enveloped her, momentarily transporting her back to happier times. She'd bought cakes from this place in the past on the recommendation of her elderly neighbour Betty. Their Danish pastries never disappointed and were Lauren's favourite. The shop was a charming blend of café and bakery, with rustic wooden tables and chairs scattered around the front area.

As she approached the counter, Lauren's eyes swept across the array of baked goods displayed in the glass case. There were tempting golden croissants, jam doughnuts, plump scones, and intricately decorated cupcakes, but Lauren pushed aside the momentary distraction. That wasn't why they were there.

Lauren walked to the front of the queue and held out her warrant card. 'We'd like to speak to Dylan Fairclough. I believe he works in the bakery.'

The man behind the counter peered at her warrant card, uncertainty flickering across his face, before gesturing to the open space behind him. His eyes darted nervously between Lauren and Matt. 'You'll need to go out the back. That's where he'll be, although I didn't see him when I was there a few minutes ago.'

Lauren nodded and, together with Matt, made her way into a much larger room. The transition from cosy café to industrial bakery was marked. Several people were working various machines and the whir and clank of equipment filled the air. Tall trolleys laden with different types of bread lined the space. The employees were all dressed in white hats and overalls.

'Yes?' a woman called out, looking up from her work and heading over to them. Her face was flushed from the heat of the ovens, and a light dusting of flour covered her apron.

Lauren held out her warrant card once more, watching as the woman's eyes widened slightly. 'I'm Detective Inspector Pengelly, and this is Detective Sergeant Price. We'd like a word with Dylan Fairclough, please.'

The woman sighed. 'Sorry, love, he's not here. You've missed him by ten minutes. He received a phone call – something they're not meant to do during work time I might add – and then said he had to go out and that he was taking an early lunch.'

Lauren glanced at her watch. It was only eleven forty-five. What was so urgent that he had to head out straight away? Unease settled in her gut, a familiar sensation that often preceded trouble in a case.

'Are you the manager?' Lauren asked, her voice calm, hiding the growing tension that was bubbling.

'No. Our manager had a medical emergency so isn't here. That's why Dylan could leave without permission.'

'Do you know where he went?' Lauren asked hopefully.

The woman hesitated, her eyes darting around the room as if searching for an answer. 'I overheard him on the phone saying, "I'll meet you in the gardens at the front of the museum." I think he meant the cable museum.'

'The one at Porthcurno?' Matt asked, his eyebrows raising in surprise.

Lauren sensed his excitement at this potential lead.

'That's the only cable museum we have round here,' the woman said, with a hint of sarcasm, her flour-covered hands gesturing vaguely.

'What made you think it was there?' Lauren asked.

'Because it has some lovely gardens. I'm sorry, but I really need to get back to work, or the brioche will be ruined,' the woman said with a frustrated sigh.

Who on earth would Fairclough be meeting? The location was significant, for sure, given its proximity to where Jasmine and Finley's bodies were found.

'Do you have any idea who he was talking to on the phone?' Lauren asked, as a throw-away question because she doubted the woman did.

'From the way he was talking, I'd say it was a girl.'

'Are you sure?' Lauren asked.

'Not for certain, but men talking to each other on the phone are different, aren't they? More brash, if you get what I mean.' The woman pulled a face.

'Yes, I do,' Lauren agreed. 'Did you hear anything else? Did he mention a name when he answered by any chance?'

'I thought I heard him say *May*, but I couldn't swear to that.'

'Okay, thanks for your help. If Dylan comes back, please let him know that we need to speak to him urgently.'

'What if he asks what it's about?' the woman asked, tilting her head to one side.

'You can tell him truthfully that you don't know. I won't keep you. We don't want the brioche spoilt. Thanks for your time.' Lauren gave the woman a brief smile before turning to leave.

As they walked out of the bakery and back to the car, Lauren's head was spinning with possibilities. The fresh sea air hit her as they stepped outside, very different from the warm, yeasty atmosphere of the bakery.

Once they were seated in the car, Matt turned to her, his face etched with concern. 'I assume we're heading for the cable museum, ma'am?'

'Definitely,' Lauren replied, her determination growing. 'This is the first real connection to the deaths that we've had. But who's Fairclough meeting? Who's *May*? That's assuming the woman in the bakery heard correctly.'

'Ma'am, you don't think he could have said "Fay", do you?' Matt asked, his eyes widening slightly.

Lauren paused, considering the possibility. 'I suppose if she only heard the "a" it could have been. Why?'

'Because Fay could be short for Faith. Faith knows that we want to speak to him.' Matt paused. 'Do you think she warned him that we were on our way?'

'Why would she do that?' Lauren asked, frowning.

'What if Faith believed that Dylan Fairclough killed her brother and she's going to accuse him? Or...' Matt's words fell away, and he expelled a loud breath. 'Or even worse, what if she's going to exact her revenge for the murders?'

A chill ran down Lauren's spine. If Matt was right, they could end up with another murder on their hands. 'I've no idea but we can't risk it. We need to get there quickly.'

Matt nodded grimly. 'Shall I call for backup?'

'Good idea. Tell them to meet us at Porthcurno cable museum,' Lauren instructed. 'Also, speak to Ellie and ask her to contact the museum so they can check their cameras to see if they can identify where they are.'

'Yes, ma'am.' Matt pulled out his phone, ready to make the necessary calls.

If their hunch was right, they had to get there before Faith did anything stupid.

Lauren started the engine and headed in the direction of Porthcurno. The picturesque Cornish landscape blurred past the windows as she navigated the winding roads, going as fast as the terrain would allow.

* * *

Matt sat beside Lauren as she drove as fast as she could to reach the Porthcurno cable museum. The winding roads made it challenging to maintain a high speed, but Lauren navigated them with determination. Matt's eyes darted between the road ahead and the passing landscape but he barely noticed the beautiful scenery because he was consumed with the urgent situation at hand. Tension radiated from Lauren, mirroring his own sense of urgency.

His phone rang, cutting through the silence in the car, and after checking the screen and seeing it was Ellie, he answered and put the call on speaker.

'Hi, Ellie. What have you got for us? The DI can also hear you.'

'Sarge, ma'am,' Ellie said. 'I've been in touch with the cable museum and got them to check their CCTV footage. They have a camera on the car park and one at the entrance. There's no evidence of either of them being there. They've got three families, a couple and one single older man visiting at present. They said no one else has been there today.'

Matt clenched his fist in disappointment. Where could they be? He looked at Lauren, noticing her knuckles whitening as she gripped the steering wheel even tighter.

'We'll still head over there in case they're somewhere the cameras don't reach. Like the gardens,' Lauren said, her eyes fixed on the road ahead.

'Have you looked at the CCTV footage on the streets?' Matt asked, an idea forming. 'We're looking for two cars. Faith's and Dylan Fairclough's.'

'Not yet, ma'am, but I'll ask Clem to check,' Ellie replied.

'Thanks.'

After ending the call, he turned to Lauren. 'I hope you're right about them being in the garden because otherwise we're up the creek without a paddle.'

'Not quite. But it won't be easy,' Lauren replied.

They approached Porthcurno and the iconic white satellite dishes of the cable museum came into view. Their massive structures stood out against the landscape, a reminder of how exposed and public this meeting place was.

They parked along the main road and quickly exited the vehicle. Two police cars were already there, and several officers were waiting for them.

Lauren approached them, her usual composure showing signs of strain. 'Wait here. We might not need you,' she instructed.

'Yes, ma'am,' they replied, standing at the ready.

Matt followed Lauren. What could Faith possibly want from her brother's suspected killer? The colourful garden, with its array of bright flowers and lush green plants, seemed incongruous with having two unsolved murders hanging over them all.

As they searched the grounds, checking every possible meeting spot, the frustration built. Neither Faith nor Dylan Fairclough was there.

'Where the hell are they,' he muttered, running a hand through his hair. If Faith had information about her brother's murder, or she'd discovered something that implicated or cleared Dylan Fairclough, they needed to know.

They returned to the car park, the burden of missed opportunity pressing heavily on his shoulders.

Lauren's mouth was set in a thin line as she turned to Matt. 'Okay, they're definitely not here,' Lauren said. 'We'll go to the Glenisters' house. Faith could be there, and Fairclough might have gone elsewhere. The woman in the bakery could've been mistaken.'

'Agreed,' Matt said, already mapping out their next steps in his head. 'But we should consider reaching out to local businesses round here, in case they went somewhere else after meeting up.'

'Good idea, I'll ask the officers here to check.'

After instructing the backup officers to visit the shops and cafés, they returned to Lauren's car. Matt climbed into the passenger seat, pulled the seatbelt across his body, and clicked it into place, while Lauren started the engine and drove onto the road.

Matt stared out of the window, watching the landscape roll by. The silence of the car was heavy with questions. Why had Faith arranged this meeting? What did she know? And most importantly, if she believed Fairclough was the killer, was he in danger?

TWENTY-THREE

THURSDAY 14 SEPTEMBER

Sonia opened the door to the Glenisters' grand Regency property only seconds after Matt had rung the bell.

'How's it going in there?' Lauren asked the family liaison officer.

Sonia shook her head. 'Not good, ma'am. It's like time's stood still for all of them. Even though I regularly spend time with grieving families, it never gets easier to witness, for sure.'

'They're lucky to have you there,' Lauren said with a nod. 'We're here to see Faith,' she added, getting straight to the point.

Sonia's eyebrows shot up in surprise. 'Oh, she went out not long after you were here earlier.'

Lauren caught Matt's eye as he straightened up attentively. A surge of anticipation ran through him. This virtually confirmed that she was with Dylan Fairclough. If only they could find out where.

'Did she say where she was going?' Matt asked.

'No,' Sonia said. 'All she told me was that she needed some fresh air. Although, having said that, I did notice that she was in her car when she left, so she's not getting much fresh air. Unless she drove somewhere and then went for a walk.'

'Did you tell her parents?' Matt asked.

'No, I didn't.' Sonia looked at Matt and then Lauren, a frown crossing her usually relaxed features.

'And you didn't phone her to see where she'd gone?' Lauren pressed.

'No. Why would I? This isn't a prison,' Sonia said defensively. Was it because she was feeling challenged and didn't like it? 'What's this all about? Surely she's not a suspect?'

Matt sucked in some air, trying to remain calm as the gravity of the situation sank in. 'We believe she might have arranged to meet up with Dylan Fairclough because she thinks he's the murderer. We thought they might have gone to Porthcurno's cable museum, but when we got there, they were nowhere to be seen.'

'Do you think she's going to harm him?' Sonia asked, worry shining from her eyes.

'We don't know,' Lauren said, glancing up the stairs. 'Where's her bedroom? We'd like to take a look.'

Sonia hesitated a moment before replying. 'Third room on the left I believe.'

Lauren nodded. 'Please let the parents know we're here, and that we're having a quick look at Faith's room. We'll speak to them before we leave.'

They hurried up the stairs, Matt leading the way, his heart pounding in his chest. The plush carpet muffled their footsteps, but to Matt, the sound of his own breathing seemed deafening in the quiet house. He headed into Faith's large bedroom and quickly assessed it. It was fairly tidy, with theatre posters on the walls, books scattered on the desk, and a closed laptop on the bed. There were several framed photos on the windowsill, one of Faith standing on a stage with a group of people, and two of Faith in a judo uniform with medals around her neck. He hadn't known she was into martial arts.

'I'll start with the wardrobe and you do the dressing table,' Lauren said.

Matt headed over, but before opening the centre drawer, something behind the unit caught his eye. He leant over, pulled out a large sketchpad, and flipped it open.

'Hey, ma'am, look at this,' he called out, his voice filled with anticipation. 'It looks like Faith's as talented as Alfie Hackett, only her sketches are all of Jasmine Dodd.'

Lauren walked over as he began flipping through the pages, peering over his shoulder. 'She's very good,' Lauren murmured.

Unease twisted in Matt's gut. Something wasn't right. The sketches were beautiful, but there was an intensity to them that made him uncomfortable. 'I'll take this with us,' he said, sliding the sketchpad into an evidence bag, sealing it, and placing it on the bed.

He returned his attention to the drawers in the dressing table. Opening the first one, he rummaged through and found a small notebook, which he opened.

'Oh...' was the only word that came out of his mouth as he stared at some more sketches.

They showed Dylan Fairclough in five different poses, each one meticulously anatomically detailed. Matt's veins turned to ice as he noticed the repeated depiction of a knife plunged into the young man's chest, deep red blood pooling around the wounds. Someone had spent hours getting every detail exactly right.

'What is it?' Lauren asked, turning to face him.

'This is worse than we thought,' he said, showing Lauren the drawings, as he began unravelling the threads to what he'd discovered. 'I think we've got this totally wrong. Based on this I'd say that Faith was in love with Jasmine and now following our interview she has confirmation of what she'd previously suspected, that Dylan Fairclough had a thing for Jasmine, too.'

Lauren nodded. 'I think you're right. Thanks to us, Faith

believes that Dylan murdered the couple because he couldn't have Jasmine.'

Matt screwed up his eyes for a second. 'Crap. What have we done, ma'am?'

Lauren's face paled as the pieces appeared to click into place. 'All I said was that we haven't yet eliminated him. But that was clearly enough for her to take matters into her own hands. We need to find them. And fast. Dylan Fairclough's life is in danger.'

They hurried downstairs and burst into the drawing room, startling the Glenisters.

'Mr and Mrs Glenister,' Lauren said, her words tumbling out rapidly, 'we need to find Faith urgently. We think she might be with Dylan—'

'Dylan?' Mr Glenister cut in, his brow furrowed. 'Finley's friend?'

'Yes,' Lauren replied, trying not to sound impatient. 'We need to find them immediately.'

'I'll phone her,' Mrs Glenister said, reaching over to the coffee table and picking up her phone. They waited in silence while she pressed one of the keys. 'It's gone to voicemail,' she said after a short time.

'Is there anywhere you can think of that Faith might go when she wants to get away from it all?' Lauren asked.

Mrs Glenister thought for a moment and her hands twisted nervously in her lap. 'We have a small beach house in Porthleven that the family uses sometimes. She might have gone there. It's in Loe Bar Road.'

'How far away is it?' Matt asked, already jumping ahead, calculating travel times and potential scenarios.

'Not too far, about a twenty-five-minute drive,' Mr Glenister replied quickly.

Matt nodded decisively. 'We need the address and a set of keys, please.'

'They're on the hook in the kitchen; I'll fetch them for you,' Mrs Glenister said as she hurried out of the room.

She returned a moment later, her face stricken. 'The keys aren't there. Faith must have taken them.'

Matt's heart sank further. This was looking more and more like a premeditated act. 'Do you have a spare set?'

'Yes, I've got one to the front door,' Mr Glenister said as he pulled out a fob with several keys attached from his pocket. He took off one of them and handed it to Matt. 'But I don't understand, why is it so urgent you see Faith? And how can you be sure that she's with Dylan?'

Lauren shared a loaded glance with Matt before replying. 'We really need to speak with them. Please don't worry, Sonia's here and we'll make sure to update her with any news when we have it.'

'I want to go with you,' Mr Glenister said, standing.

'Sorry, but we need you to stay here, in case Faith returns,' Lauren said kindly.

'But I'll be here,' Mrs Glenister said. 'And so will Sonia.'

'Please, Mr and Mrs Glenister. I understand your concerns, but you need to leave this to us. This is a police investigation and it won't help if you get in the way,' Lauren said, her tone leaving no room for any dissent.

With that, they quickly took their leave. The cool sea air hit Matt, making a marked difference from the stuffy atmosphere inside the house. He pulled out his phone. 'I'll call it in. I assume you want backup to meet us there.'

'Yes, please,' Lauren agreed.

Matt made the call and then texted the beach house address to the team, his fingers flying over the screen. His mind was spinning, jumping to darker and darker conclusions about what Faith might be planning to do to Dylan Fairclough.

TWENTY-FOUR

THURSDAY 14 SEPTEMBER

Lauren put her foot down, driving as fast as she could to Porthleven, going over and over in her head the worst-case scenarios.

'But how would Faith even manage to hurt Dylan?' Lauren said, voicing out loud the thought that had been nagging at her. 'He must be twice her size.'

Matt shifted in the passenger seat. 'Actually, she's more dangerous than she looks, ma'am. There were some photos of her wearing a judo uniform, with medals around her neck, on the windowsill in her room.'

'That doesn't make me feel any better,' Lauren shot back. 'It could turn really nasty. If Dylan Fairclough is guilty of the murders, he needs to be dealt with through the courts and not at the hands of a vigilante. Especially not one with combat training.'

'But remember, she can also protect herself from him, if he turns on her,' Matt added.

'I suppose so,' Lauren acknowledged.

She continued driving, barely registering the beauty as they sped along the winding coastal road where the lush green fields gave way to rugged cliffs, with glimpses of the churning sea below. She was acutely aware of the ticking clock, with each second potentially bringing Fairclough or Faith closer to danger.

When they arrived at the white-washed house, Jenna, Clem and Billy were already there, standing beside their car. Their faces were grim and alert. The house overlooked the ocean and was in a secluded spot perched on a small cliff with a winding path leading down to the beach. There were several houses a short distance away, but they all seemed quiet and deserted.

Lauren stepped out of the car, the salty sea air hitting her face. She took a deep breath, trying to centre herself. The crash of waves against the rocks below provided a constant backdrop of sound, almost drowning out the pounding of her own heart. She scanned the area, her detective's instincts on high alert. Every shadow, every movement caught her attention.

Two cars sat in the driveway. One was Faith's, a small red hatchback, and the other she assumed belonged to Dylan Fairclough, a slightly battered blue Corsa. Lauren's insides clenched at the sight. The evidence of their presence made the danger terrifyingly real.

She turned to the others. 'Right. Keep an eye out, make sure no one comes out and gets away. Matt and I are going to knock on the door.'

Jenna, Clem, and Billy all nodded, spreading out to cover the perimeter of the property. Lauren waited until they'd taken up their positions and then strode up to the front door with Matt close behind her. The gravel crunched under their feet, sounding unnaturally loud in the silence.

Lauren knocked forcefully, the noise echoing in the stillness. But there was no answer, so she tried the handle and the door swung open easily. It was unlocked. Her sense of foreboding grew and a chill ran down her spine despite the warmth of the day.

She and Matt cautiously entered the house, their senses on

high alert. An eerie silence greeted them as they stepped
straight into the lounge. The air inside was stuffy and still,
unlike the fresh sea breeze outside. Lauren's eyes darted
around, taking in every detail. There was no sign of anyone
having been there recently.

'There's no one here,' Lauren murmured, trying to calm her
racing thoughts. 'Let's take a quick look around.'

They hurried through the rooms, checking the lounge,
dining room, kitchen. All empty. Lauren's anxiety mounted
with each vacant room. Where were they? What had Faith
done? The questions swirled in her mind, each more unsettling
than the last.

'Upstairs,' she said tersely, taking the steps two at a time.
They burst into each bedroom, finding them equally deserted.
Lauren wanted to scream in frustration. The neat, untouched
beds and tidy rooms seemed to mock their urgent search.

Back downstairs, they returned to the kitchen and Lauren
was about to suggest they check outside, when something
caught her eye. The door to the utility room was slightly open
and she could see a glass of water sitting on the worktop, half-
finished.

'Someone's been here,' Lauren said, pointing to the glass.

They stepped inside the room for a closer look and Lauren
spotted an open packet of biscuits.

'What do you think happened?' Matt asked, his face serious. 'Did Faith ask Fairclough to meet her here without telling
him why and now she's taken him somewhere?'

'It certainly looks that way. Or he's taken her. We need to
find them and—'

'Ma'am. Sarge. Quick. Out here.'

A shout from Billy propelled Lauren and Matt out of the
house. The team was clustered at the edge of the property, their
gazes fixed on the beach below. The sun was starting to dip

towards the horizon, casting long shadows across the sand. Lauren squinted against the glare, following Billy's pointing finger. Her heart leapt into her throat as she spotted two distant figures walking along the shore. It was Faith and Dylan.

'That's them, isn't it?' Matt asked, shading his eyes against the sun.

Lauren nodded, possibilities whirling around her head. 'Yes. We need to move. Now.' From their vantage point, it appeared that Faith and Dylan were having a casual walk. There weren't any signs of distress. But looks could be deceiving.

'We need to follow without alerting them to the fact that we're there. At the moment it all looks fine and neither of them seem to be in any immediate danger. But we don't know what Faith has planned for him.'

'I doubt she could do much to him at her size,' Billy said. 'I'd be more worried about what he could do to her.'

'We believe she's a martial arts expert, so don't count on it,' Matt said. 'Because one thing's for certain, she's got something up her sleeve. Or why would she have brought him here?'

The team nodded, their faces set with determination. They hurried down to the beach and split up, fanning out to tail the pair at a discreet distance.

The sand shifted under Lauren's feet, making each step a challenge. She could taste salt on her lips and hear the cry of seagulls overhead. Every sense seemed heightened by the tension of the moment.

Drawing closer to the pair, Lauren was able to make out the looks on their faces. Dylan appeared confused and his brow furrowed as he listened to Faith, who had a wildness in her eyes. There was a manic energy in her movements that set Lauren's teeth on edge.

Lauren gauged the distance and calculated the best time to make a move. She needed to be a bit closer. The sound of the

174 SALLY RIGBY

waves seemed to fade away as she narrowed in on the two
figures ahead of her.

Suddenly Faith whirled around to face Fairclough, something glinting in her hand. Lauren's blood ran cold as she recognised the unmistakable shape of a gun. Time seemed to slow
down, each second stretching into eternity as Lauren's training
kicked in.

'No.' The shout tore from Lauren's throat as she broke into a
sprint, sand spraying beneath her pounding feet. 'Police. Faith,
drop the gun.'

Faith spun to face her, while at the same time grabbing Fairclough and yanking him in front of her like a human shield. The
barrel of the gun was pressed to his temple. He yelped in fear,
his face a mask of terror. Lauren's heart raced, while she frantically searched for a way to defuse the situation.

'Faith, let him go. Please. This isn't the way.' Lauren
skidded to a stop a few metres away, sand flying around her feet.
'Drop the gun, now.'

'No,' Faith shrieked, an edge of hysteria in her voice. 'You
don't understand. He must pay for what he did.'

Faith pressed the gun harder against Fairclough's head and
he whimpered. His face was ashen and exuded fear. Lauren
had to find a way to end this before Faith pulled the trigger.

'Faith, listen to me,' she said, fighting to keep her voice calm.
'If you hurt Dylan, there's no coming back from that. It won't
change what happened to Jasmine and Finley. It will only make
things worse for you. Please, don't do it.'

Faith's face twisted with anguish, a kaleidoscope of
emotions flashing across her features. 'I don't care. My life's
already over.'

Lauren's emotions whirled as she contemplated a way to
reach the distraught girl. She could hear her team moving into
position behind her, but she dared not look away from Faith.

One wrong move could be catastrophic. 'Faith, I know you're in pain. But this isn't the answer. Jasmine wouldn't want this. She wouldn't want you to throw your life away.'

For a moment, Faith wavered, the gun lowering a fraction. Lauren held her breath, hardly daring to hope.

But then Faith's face hardened, her grip on the gun tightening. 'You don't know anything about Jasmine. About us. You're trying to trick me.' She started backing away, dragging a terrified Fairclough with her. The sun cast long shadows across the beach, adding an eerie quality to the strained standoff. 'Here's what's going to happen. Dylan and I are going to walk away. If any of you try to stop us, I'll kill him. I swear.'

Lauren's heart sank as she raised her hands in surrender. She couldn't risk Fairclough's life. Every instinct screamed at her to act, but she knew any sudden move could be disastrous.

'Okay, Faith. We won't stop you. But please, don't hurt him.'

Faith let out a brittle laugh, the sound chilling in its lack of mirth. 'That's up to him. If he does what I say, he'll be fine. Won't you, Dylan?'

Dylan nodded frantically, tears streaming down his face. 'I'll do whatever you want, Faith. Please, please don't shoot me.'

'Good boy. Let's go,' Faith said with a chilling smile that didn't reach her eyes.

Faith started backing away, keeping the gun trained on Dylan's head, while Lauren watched on helplessly as they disappeared into the dunes. Every cell in Lauren's body screamed at her to do something, anything. But she couldn't act. Not without risking Dylan's life. Frustration and despair warred within her as she turned to the others, seeing her own helplessness mirrored on their faces.

'We can't let her get away,' Matt said urgently. 'Who knows what she'll do to him.'

Lauren nodded. 'We won't. But we must be clever about

this. We'll follow them at a distance, staying out of sight, and wait for an opening. There's bound to be one.'

It went against every instinct she had, but they had no choice. Faith was unstable and armed. One wrong move could prove fatal for Dylan.

TWENTY-FIVE
THURSDAY 14 SEPTEMBER

Matt's heart hammered against his ribs as he and Lauren crouched behind the dune, salt-laden wind whipping across their faces. His eyes remained locked on Faith's retreating figure, willing her not to turn around. She marched determinedly along the beach towards the house, the gun glinting ominously in her hand. The sun cast long shadows across the sand and painted the sky in brilliant hues of orange and pink. On any other day, it would have been a scene of breathtaking beauty. Now it felt like nature's cruel joke, beauty masking the horror unfolding before them.

He risked a sideways peek at Lauren. Her face was a mask of concentration and her body coiled so tightly it could almost snap. Even her breathing seemed calculated and measured, as if each inhale might give away their position.

'Backup's on the way,' Lauren whispered, her voice barely carrying over the soft rush of waves. 'But we *can't* lose sight of them.'

Something in that emphasis made Matt's spine crawl.

'Where on earth did she get the gun?' Matt muttered, his mouth dry. 'Assuming it's real, of course.'

Lauren shrugged, her eyes never wavering from their target. 'That's something we'll have to find out, but from where I stood it looked to be.'

Matt swallowed hard, his throat clicking. 'I can't believe we missed this. She seemed so... dispirited.'

Lauren's eyes flickered to Matt for a moment. 'That's exactly what makes her dangerous. The most desperate are those who've got nothing left to lose.'

They kept following, their footsteps muffled by the soft sand. The crash of waves provided cover for their pursuit, but Matt's nerves were on edge. Every movement and every sound could potentially alert Faith to their presence, except she never looked back once to see if they were in pursuit. Instead she kept on walking with her arm linked through Dylan's as if they were simply taking a stroll. Maybe she didn't care because she knew they wouldn't do anything while she was armed.

Matt's hand instinctively moved towards his hip, where a gun would be if they were armed. Which of course they weren't. This wasn't America, although for once he wished it was.

Eventually, they arrived back at the house and Matt watched Faith as she scanned the area, her expression unreadable. She must have seen them all in the distance but it didn't appear to concern her. She pushed Dylan into the passenger seat of her car and then got in herself, driving off so fast that dust and dirt billowed up from the road, momentarily hiding her from them.

'Go, go, go,' Lauren shouted, her voice sharp with urgency.

The team sprinted back to the vehicles and they began following Faith, with Lauren in the lead. She kept their distance while navigating the narrow, winding roads of the Cornish countryside.

Matt gripped the dashboard as Lauren took a sharp turn, the tyres screeching. 'We can't lose her,' he muttered, more to himself than to Lauren. His eyes scanned the road ahead, searching for any sign of Faith's car.

'We won't,' Lauren said with determination.

Every muscle in Matt's body tensed as their car hugged each bend. The chase continued through the rolling hills and rugged cliffs, while Faith's car swerved and dodged, trying to lose them, but Lauren kept up.

'She's heading for the coastal road,' Matt exclaimed, pointing ahead. 'If she gets there, we might lose her in the traffic.'

'We won't let that happen.' Lauren pressed her foot harder on the accelerator, her entire body taut.

What was Faith's next move going to be? Would she try to lose them by heading down one of the many narrow, unmarked roads? Or would she head for the cliffs, hoping to make a daring escape? They had to be ready for anything.

'What's her endgame here?' Matt said, his fingers drumming nervously on his thigh.

Lauren shook her head slightly. 'I don't know. But whatever it is, we need to stop her before someone gets hurt.'

Suddenly, Faith's car screeched to a halt at a junction and she narrowly missed hitting a car driving along the main road. Lauren pulled up behind her at the same time as the passenger door opened and Dylan threw himself out, his face pale and frightened.

Without hesitation, Matt leapt from the car, leaving Lauren behind the wheel. He ran over to Faith's car, his breath coming in short bursts, and jumped inside, snatching the gun from her lap and throwing it outside. He then seized the steering wheel with one hand and grabbed hold of Faith's arm with the other.

'Get off me,' Faith screamed, her voice shrill with panic. She thrashed wildly, her elbow catching Matt in the ribs. He grunted in pain but wouldn't let go, his muscles straining with the effort.

'It's over, Faith,' Matt grunted, struggling to keep her under control. 'Don't make this worse for yourself.'

Faith's eyes were wild, darting around like a cornered animal. 'You don't understand,' she yelled, still fighting against Matt's grip. 'None of you understand.'

Lauren arrived at the driver's side, yanked open the door and pulled Faith out of the car, her expression fierce. Faith stumbled, nearly falling, but Lauren kept a firm grip on her arm. She glanced at Matt. 'Are you okay?'

'Yes, ma'am,' Matt confirmed.

Lauren turned back to the young woman in her grasp. 'Faith Glenister, I'm arresting you for the abduction of Dylan Fairclough,' she stated, her voice ringing out in the sudden stillness.

'He killed Jasmine and Finley,' Faith protested, her eyes wide with panic. She twisted in Lauren's grasp, trying to break free. 'I had to find out the truth.' Her voice rose in desperation.

'You do not have to say anything but it may harm your defence if you do not mention when questioned something which you later rely on in court. Anything you do say may be given in evidence,' Lauren finished as she handcuffed Faith, her movements swift and precise.

'I had to,' Faith repeated, her voice breaking. She suddenly went limp, as if all the fight had drained out of her. Matt and Lauren traded a wary glance, both knowing that this sudden change could be a ruse.

As they escorted Faith to one of the police cars that had arrived, she made one last desperate attempt to escape. She threw her weight backwards, catching Matt off guard. He stumbled, nearly losing his grip on her arm.

'Faith, stop,' Matt shouted, regaining his balance and tightening his hold. 'It's over. Don't make this any worse for yourself.'

Faith's shoulders slumped in defeat as they reached the police car. As she was placed in the back seat, Matt caught a glimpse of her face. The wild, manic energy was gone, replaced by a look of utter despair. For a moment, he felt a pang of sympathy for her, even after what she'd done.

After Faith was driven away, Matt turned his attention to Fairclough, who was still standing by the roadside, looking dazed. Matt approached him with measured steps.

'Are you okay, Dylan?' Matt asked firmly.

The young man's eyes were wide and his breathing rapid. He looked at Matt, then at Lauren, who had joined them. 'Yes... yes... I think so,' he stammered. 'She... Faith... she said she wanted to talk about Finley and Jasmine. I never thought... the gun...' His voice trailed off, and he swayed slightly on his feet.

Matt stayed alert, watching Fairclough's every move, in case he tried to get away. 'Did she hurt you?'

Fairclough winced slightly and touched the side of his body. 'She elbowed me in the ribs and twisted my arm up my back when I tried to get away earlier.'

Lauren's expression remained impartial. 'We'll have a paramedic check you out at the station.' She turned to a nearby officer. 'PC Thompson, please escort Mr Fairclough to the station. He needs medical attention, but do not leave him alone.'

'Before you go,' Lauren said, staring at Fairclough, her eyes cold, 'I'm arresting you on suspicion of the murders of Jasmine Dodd and Finley Glenister. You do not have to say anything but it may harm your defence if you do not mention when questioned something which you later rely on in court. Anything you do say may be given in evidence. Do you understand?'

Fairclough's face paled further. 'But I didn't... I'm not...'

'Do you understand?' Lauren repeated, each word sharp as broken glass.

'Yes, but—' Fairclough's protest withered as Lauren's eyes locked onto his. A bead of sweat rolled down the side of his face.

'Take him away,' Lauren instructed the officer standing

beside her, her words carrying a finality that made Fairclough's shoulders slump.

The officer nodded as he approached Fairclough. 'Come with me, sir.'

As Dylan Fairclough was escorted to the waiting police car, his feet stumbling on the pavement, a loaded look passed between Lauren and Matt. They both knew that this was far from over.

TWENTY-SIX

THURSDAY 14 SEPTEMBER

'Here he comes, the man of the moment,' Billy said when Lauren and Matt walked into the office, his excitement palpable. 'Can you believe that Sarge saved the day again? It's like your MO. Was he like that in Lenchester, Ellie?'

Ellie blushed, still clearly uncomfortable with the attention. The young officer's eyes darted around the room, looking anywhere but at Billy. 'Umm...'

'Answer Billy's question, Ellie. Or he won't stop going on about it. And, by the way, just so you all know, the gun was a replica, so I wasn't in any danger,' Matt said, stepping in, his tone light but firm.

Lauren smiled to herself at the way her sergeant was able to defuse the excitement without sounding patronising.

'But you didn't know that, did you?' Billy persisted, his admiration for Matt evident. 'Well, Ellie? Tell us everything.'

'Okay. All I can tell you is that Sarge wasn't one to bottle it when things got rough... if you get what I mean,' Ellie said, finally relenting, a smile hovering on the edge of her mouth.

'I knew it,' Billy said, smirking. 'And what about—'

'Okay, okay, enough of Sergeant Price's adulation, however

much it's warranted,' Lauren said, holding up her hand to silence the young officer. She needed the team to focus on what was important: solving Jasmine and Finley's murders. Until it was all sorted, they couldn't afford to be sidetracked by office banter. 'We're interviewing Dylan Fairclough first, and then Faith Glenister. Although I've charged Fairclough with murder, all we have is circumstantial evidence. We need proof if this is going to stick. I still want you all to dig into his background and check CCTV for his whereabouts around the time of the murders. When we first spoke to him, he mentioned texting Finley during the Saturday evening. Ellie, is that correct?'

'Yes, ma'am, they did text about meeting up in the week. Surely he wouldn't have done that if he planned to murder the couple later?' Ellie replied, looking puzzled.

'He might, if he wanted an alibi,' Billy said.

'Or he might not have decided to kill them at that stage,' Clem added. 'Or he wanted everything to appear normal to the couple and not alert them.'

'Any of those suggestions would fit,' Lauren said. 'If anything further comes up let me know. If we want him to admit to the murders, the more we can throw at him the better. Right, come on, Matt. Let's go.'

Determination coursed through Lauren as they reached the interview room and she sucked in a deep breath, steeling herself for what was to come. Dylan Fairclough was seated, his face pale, his eyes bloodshot and his legs shaking. He looked vulnerable and broken, against the stark white walls of the interview room.

His body language clearly revealed his anxiety. But was he ready to confess?

She nodded to Matt to start the recording, and the soft whir of the recorder filled the silence.

'Interview on Thursday, 14 September. Those present: Detective Inspector Pengelly, Detective Sergeant Price, and—'

Matt looked directly at Fairclough. 'Please state your name for the recording.'

His voice, barely above a whisper, cracked slightly as he spoke. 'Dylan Alexander Fairclough.'

Lauren leant forward, her elbows resting on the table. 'Right, Mr Fairclough, before we start, I'd like to confirm that you've received medical attention and are fine to be interviewed.'

'Yeah. I'm okay.'

'Also that you refused legal representation when offered it.'

'I don't want any,' Fairclough muttered angrily. 'I haven't done anything.'

That meant nothing. Lauren had conducted countless interviews where the suspect was guilty and refused representation.

'If that's the case, then why do you think that Faith Glenister came after you?'

'How am I meant to know?' he asked, shooting her a scathing look.

'You don't think it could be because she knew that you murdered her brother and Jasmine Dodd?' Lauren asked, raising an eyebrow.

'But I didn't.' A bead of sweat formed on Fairclough's brow.

'Did she accuse you of the murders?'

Dylan ran a hand through his hair, his eyes darting around the room like a trapped animal. 'Not exactly. She was out of it and not being... I don't know what she was doing. She seemed very upset. Kept muttering about Jasmine and Finley, about how unfair it all was. But she didn't outright accuse me.'

'She implied it, though,' Matt suggested.

'I don't know. Maybe. I'm not sure.'

Lauren decided to change tack. 'Do you think it was because Faith discovered you were infatuated with Jasmine and had tried to persuade her to leave Finley for you?'

Fairclough's eyes widened and he jerked back in his chair as if he'd been slapped. 'How do you know that?'

'We found the box of *trinkets* in your bedroom. Photos of Jasmine, items which we assume belong to her. How did you get all these things?'

Fairclough shrugged. 'I took some of the photos. The other items... I've been collecting them for a long time.'

'Did Jasmine know you had them?'

'I don't know. But so what, it doesn't mean anything. They're just things.'

'We've also read the letters you sent to Jasmine. What do you have to say about that?' Lauren asked, tilting her head to one side.

'Okay, so I liked Jasmine. The last time I checked it's not illegal.'

'Unlike stalking your teacher, Eva Millington,' Lauren countered.

'B-but—' Fairclough spluttered, his face crimson.

'But nothing,' Lauren retorted. 'You have a history of obsessive behaviour. What I'd like to know is whether you became obsessed with your teacher because of the striking resemblance to Jasmine or whether it was the other way round? Whether you diverted your affections onto Eva Millington because you couldn't have Jasmine.'

'I've loved Jasmine since we first met when we were thirteen.'

'So Eva Millington was instead of Jasmine, although you didn't home in on her until Jasmine started seeing Finley, is that correct?'

Fairclough closed his eyes for a few seconds. 'Yeah, I suppose so.'

'What I don't understand is why didn't you admit your feelings to Jasmine until you were much older,' Lauren said.

'Once she'd started going out with Finley, I couldn't keep it a secret.'

'I see. It's our opinion, Dylan, that you were so angry at the thought of them getting engaged that you decided to end it for them both. If you couldn't have Jasmine, then no one could.'

'You're wrong,' Fairclough replied sounding desperate. His hands gripped the edge of the table. He was getting more worked up. 'Finley was my best friend.'

'So you claim,' Lauren said, her voice level but her gaze intense. 'Yet you pursued his girlfriend. How do you reconcile those two things? What did you think would have happened to your friendship if you'd succeeded in taking Jasmine from him?'

'You don't understand. Jasmine should have been mine. I loved her way before Finley even knew she existed.' Fairclough's voice rose angrily.

'And you thought that gave you permission to still go after her?' Matt interjected, his tone sharp.

Fairclough's shoulders slumped, as if all the fight had drained out of him. 'I'm devastated that they're both dead, but I had nothing to do with it. You have to believe me.'

'Have you ever been prescribed sleeping pills?' Lauren asked.

'No,' Fairclough responded.

'What about any member of your family?'

'I don't know. Why?' Fairclough frowned.

'Jasmine and Finley had been drugged.'

Fairclough's eyes widened. 'Well it wasn't me, I promise.'

'Okay... Where were you on Saturday night between eight-thirty and midnight?' Lauren asked, looking directly at the man.

Fairclough blinked furiously. 'Um...'

'Come on, Dylan, it was only a few days ago,' Lauren cajoled.

She noticed Matt watching the discussion intently, his brow furrowed.

'I... I...' His voice cracked.

'You what?' Lauren said sharply. 'Where were you?'

'I'll tell you but it's not what you think,' Fairclough muttered, while he looked anywhere but directly at Lauren, his shoulders hunched and his hands fidgeting with a loose thread on his sleeve.

'I'm waiting,' Lauren said, her voice cold.

'I was parked opposite Jasmine's house and watched Finley pick her up and then followed them to Porthcurno Beach. I wanted to watch him propose, without them knowing I was there.' Fairclough's words tumbled out in a rush, and his leg bounced nervously under the table, causing it to shake. 'But when it came to it, I couldn't face it. So I went home.'

Lauren's phone pinged. It was a text from Jenna.

Fairclough's mum's car in the vicinity of the murders on Saturday.

Lauren hurriedly replied.

Thanks. Check with neighbours if anyone saw the car arrive back.

'Were you in your mum's car?' Lauren asked, looking up from her phone and studying the young man's face.

Fairclough started and his hand jerked, knocking over an empty plastic cup on the table. 'Yes. How do you know?'

'You were seen on CCTV. Why use her car?'

'I didn't want Fin and Jasmine to spot me.' Fairclough's eyes darted around the room, never settling on one spot for long.

'What time did Finley and Jasmine leave her house?' Lauren asked, wanting to establish the timeline.

'They left at about half-past eight and arrived at the beach twenty-five minutes later.'

'And once you got there, did you then go to the beach and drink some prosecco with them to celebrate?' Lauren pushed.

'No. I've already told you I didn't stay. I couldn't face it and left a few minutes after nine and went home.' He swiped away the bead of sweat that had formed on his temple.

If he was telling the truth then he wasn't there during the time of death Henry had indicated. But Lauren wasn't convinced.

'Let me get this straight, Dylan. You followed Jasmine and Finley to Porthcurno Beach, parked your car and watched them head down the steps onto the sand, and then you chickened out and went home without them ever knowing you were there.'

Fairclough nodded. 'Yeah.'

'If you were in my position, would you think that was true, Dylan? Because I'm having a hard time believing it. Especially considering you have a motive for seeing the pair of them dead.'

Fairclough banged his hands on the table. 'Look, I'm telling you the truth. I don't care what you think.'

'What time did you arrive home?' Lauren asked, deliberately ignoring the outburst.

'Around half-nine, I think.'

'Can anyone vouch for you? Your parents, perhaps?' Lauren asked.

'No. They were at a wedding.'

'Neighbours?'

Fairclough shrugged, his shoulders rising and falling in an exaggerated motion. 'I don't know.'

'You understand how this looks, don't you?'

'I don't know.' Fairclough's voice was barely above a whisper and his Adam's apple bobbed as he swallowed hard, the fight having left him.

'Well, let me tell you again. You drove out to the place where a woman you were obsessed with was getting engaged to someone, which meant your chance of being with her had totally disappeared. If you couldn't have her, then nobody could.' Lauren inched forward, her fingers laced together and resting on the table.

'No, that's not it at all.'

'The evidence we've gathered points strongly in your direction,' Lauren said, keeping her tone impersonal. 'You tell us that you were home by around nine-thirty yet no one can vouch for you. Why don't you admit you murdered Jasmine and Finley? Honesty at this stage of the investigation will go in your favour.'

'I'm not going to admit to something I didn't do. Why don't you ask Faith about it? Just because she came after me with a gun doesn't make her innocent.'

'The gun wasn't real. It was a replica,' Lauren explained. 'Are you now saying that Faith murdered her brother and Jasmine? Because we have no evidence to suggest that she was involved.'

Fairclough hesitated, his fingers drumming nervously on the table. The sound echoed in the small room. 'Faith was in love with Jasmine, too, you know.'

'Yes, we're aware of that. Were you surprised by that admission?' Lauren asked, watching his face closely.

'Well, yes and no, I suppose,' he stumbled, his face colouring. 'I know Faith's had boyfriends in the past, but nothing serious. And she's always talked a lot about Jasmine. Almost too much. I assumed it was because she liked her a lot as a friend. But now I know it was more than that.'

'Did Faith tell you how she felt about Jasmine getting engaged to Finley?' Lauren asked, as what she would have previously thought to be unthinkable came to the forefront of her mind.

'She said she couldn't bear the thought of it. She was... she was crying, saying it should have been her. She told me that her life was over.'

Lauren glanced at Matt, who was also watching Fairclough intently, his expression mirroring her own.

Had they got this wrong?

Lauren marched into the main office with Matt close behind. They stood next to the whiteboard and she scanned the room. 'Attention, everyone,' she demanded. 'We have a development.'

With the exception of Clem, who was speaking on the phone, all eyes were on her.

'What is it?' Billy asked, leaning forward on his desk.

'First of all, any joy on the alibis for Dylan Fairclough and Alfie Hackett?' she asked, hoping to at least eliminate one of them from their enquiries.

'One of the neighbours thought they saw Fairclough's mother's car parked in the drive around ten-fifteen on Saturday night but they're not a hundred percent. We need to investigate further,' Jenna said.

Lauren exhaled loudly. 'Thanks. And Hackett?'

'I believe Clem's talking to someone about that, ma'am,' Jenna said, at the same time as the officer ended his call.

Clem grimaced at Lauren, a despondent expression on his face. 'Ma'am, I chased up the manager from the Red Lion pub because he hadn't got back to me, and he confirmed that Alfie

Hackett was there on Saturday night. He couldn't have murdered the couple. So that puts him out of the frame and leaves Fairclough. Although if he was home by ten-fifteen it makes the time frame between murdering the couple and driving back very tight.'

'Crap,' Billy moaned. 'If neither of them did it then we're back to square one.'

'Not exactly,' Matt said, looking at Lauren. She nodded, as confirmation that he could deliver the news to the team. 'We have a new suspect. Faith Glenister.'

'What?' Jenna exclaimed, her eyes wide. 'You're kidding, right? I mean, no way would she murder her brother? Aren't they close? She tried to get Hackett to stop hounding him for money, remember.'

'No, Jenna, we're not kidding,' Lauren said. 'Faith's love for Jasmine matched that of Fairclough's. But at the moment it's all circumstantial, and we certainly haven't eliminated Fairclough as a potential suspect. We're going to question Faith Glenister and while we're away I want a deep dive into her. All hands on deck. Her mobile's in the custody suite, so Ellie, please will you start on that. Also relook at the couple's texts, paying attention to any interactions they had with Faith – in particular, disagreements between her and her brother that we'd maybe overlooked before.'

Lauren left the office with Matt and headed down to the interview room where Faith Glenister had been placed after being processed.

'Hello, Faith,' Lauren said as they entered.

The fluorescent lights cast harsh shadows across the small, utilitarian space and the young woman was seated, slumped over the table with her head resting on her arms. The sight of her, so defeated and small, made Lauren's heart twinge with unexpected sympathy. But that wasn't going to stop her from carrying out a thorough investigation. Especially as she was now a suspect.

Faith glanced up at Lauren and Matt and then sat upright but didn't reply to Lauren's greeting. Her eyes were red-rimmed and her cheeks blotchy. She flattened her dishevelled hair with a swipe of her hand and let out a long, ragged breath.

Once they were seated opposite Faith, Lauren nodded to Matt to start the recording.

'Interview on 14 September. Those present: Detective Inspector Pengelly, Detective Sergeant Price, and— Please state your name for the recording,' Matt said.

The young woman appeared determined to avoid eye contact with either of them, and fixed her gaze on a spot on the table. She muttered something unintelligible, her shoulders hunched, as if trying to make herself smaller.

'Faith, please state your name for the recording,' Lauren prompted, keeping her tone neutral. She moved forward slightly, trying to catch Faith's eye.

Faith again muttered something which couldn't be heard, her fingers tracing invisible patterns on the table's surface.

'Please speak up,' Lauren said, barely able to keep the frustration from her voice.

'Faith Colleen Glenister,' she finally said, raising her head slightly. Her voice wasn't very loud but, in the quiet room, it could be heard.

'Thank you,' Lauren replied. 'We have a few questions for you regarding today. Why did you arrange to meet with Dylan Fairclough?' Lauren shifted her position and the chair creaked.

'Because... you said he was involved Jasmine and Finley's deaths and I wanted to ask him about it.' Faith's voice broke when she stated the victims' names and a flicker of pain crossed her face.

Was this an example of Faith's acting ability or was she

telling the truth? If she was then their belief that she committed the murders was wrong.

'What were you planning to do? Kill him?' Lauren asked bluntly, observing Faith's reaction closely.

'No.' Faith's head jerked up and for the first time she met Lauren's gaze directly. 'I wanted to find out why he did it.'

Very convenient. But Lauren wasn't going to be taken in. She'd seen too many suspects try to talk their way out of trouble.

'If that was the case, then why do it in that way? Why run off when we arrived?' Lauren pressed, her voice hardening. 'I'm sure you realise how it looks from our perspective.'

The fluorescent light flickered momentarily, and Faith blinked several times.

'I wanted to speak to Dylan on my own. I knew that once you had him, I'd never get to know the truth, which was all I wanted.' Faith kept her eyes lowered, no longer making eye contact. 'It was *my* brother and *my* friend who were murdered. I had to know why he did it.' Her voice trembled slightly, anger and grief colouring her words.

The tension radiated off the young woman. There was definitely more to the story. Lauren could almost feel the heaviness of the unsaid words hanging in the air between them.

'And the gun? Why did you have that with you?' Lauren asked, her tone sharp.

Faith shrugged, a gesture that made Lauren want to shake her.

'It seemed a good idea at the time, but I suppose it was a stupid thing to do.'

'You're right, it was,' Lauren agreed. 'It caused a lot of trouble.'

'But it wasn't real,' Faith said, a defensive tone creeping into her voice.

'We know *now* that it was a replica. But we didn't at the

time and had to act accordingly,' Matt interjected, his calm voice a counterpoint to Lauren's growing frustration.

'Yeah, I suppose you didn't,' Faith admitted.

'You still haven't answered my question regarding why you brought it with you,' Lauren said. 'Were you going to threaten Dylan? Force him to tell you the truth?'

Faith hesitated, then nodded. 'I thought it would persuade him to tell me what he'd done.'

'I would have thought your martial arts proficiency would have sufficed, if you wanted Dylan to do as you asked,' Matt said.

Faith frowned. 'Possibly, I suppose. But a gun's more threatening and immediate.'

'Where did you get it?' Lauren pressed.

'It was a prop I used in a play at school. I didn't return it and no one asked for it.'

Lauren raised an eyebrow. 'How long have you had it?'

'I don't know, maybe four or five years,' Faith said with a shrug. 'Like I said, it wasn't real.'

'But it was very realistic,' Matt pointed out.

Faith shrugged again. 'Well, yeah. That's why it was a prop.'

Lauren studied the young woman. Something wasn't adding up. The pieces of the puzzle were there, but they weren't quite fitting together. 'So, to confirm, you were planning to speak to Dylan, to get him to admit to murdering Jasmine and Finley by threatening him with a gun?'

'Yes,' Faith replied quietly, tears spilling down her cheeks, which she quickly wiped away.

'Did he admit to the killings?' Lauren asked, her fingers drumming an irregular pattern on the table.

'No. But he would've done if you hadn't come along,' Faith said, her shoulders rigid beneath her jacket.

'And then what would you have done?' Lauren asked, her fists clenching.

A mix of fear, anger and grief flickered across the girl's face, and something else: guilt?

'I don't know. I didn't think that far ahead. Maybe phone the police?' Faith's voice was flat and emotionless, but it didn't sit well next to the turmoil evident in her eyes.

This was all too convenient and Lauren wasn't buying it.

'Really? Then why didn't you hand him to us when you had the chance?'

'I don't know,' Faith repeated, her voice taking on a sullen tone. She crossed her arms defensively.

'Because you had something else in mind?' Lauren snapped, her patience finally wearing thin. The words echoed in the small room, seeming to hang in the air between them.

'I don't know,' Faith responded for a third time, glaring at Lauren, her defiance shining through.

'You don't seem to know much,' Lauren replied sharply. Her impatience was building, and the desire to shake the truth out of the woman was almost overwhelming.

Matt nudged her foot under the table. A silent warning. Lauren took a deep breath, forcing herself to calm down. He was right, they weren't going to get anywhere if they kept antagonising Faith. Lauren nodded slightly to acknowledge his intervention.

Matt cleared his throat. 'When we looked around your room—'

'You were in my bedroom?' Faith interrupted, her eyes widening. 'Who gave you permission?'

'Your parents,' Lauren said coolly, watching Faith's face contort with anger. She could almost feel the waves of resentment radiating off the woman.

'Bloody typical. They had to interfere.' Faith's hands clenched into fists on the table.

'As I was saying,' Matt continued, 'when we looked around

your room, we found a sketchpad hidden behind the dressing table.'

Faith's face reddened and embarrassment flashed across her features.

'So what?' Faith's attempt at indifference was belied by the tremor in her voice and the panic in her eyes.

'In the sketchpad, there were many drawings of Jasmine,' Lauren said, taking over. 'You had strong feelings for your friend, didn't you?'

'So what?' Faith repeated, but the fight had gone out of her voice. She appeared small and vulnerable, a far cry from the defiant person of moments ago.

'How did you feel when you discovered Finley and Jasmine were going to be engaged?' Lauren probed, keeping her voice low.

They were on the verge of a breakthrough and she didn't want to jeopardise it by being too confrontational.

Faith was silent for a long time and the only sound in the room was the soft hum of the recording equipment and the young woman's shaky breathing. When she spoke, her voice was barely audible. 'Okay, I wasn't happy about it.'

'Why not?' Lauren pressed.

Faith took a deep breath. 'Look... yeah, okay. I do have feelings for Jasmine. I always have done, back from when we were at school. It's just how it is. But Finley was no good for her. He was no good for anyone.' The words tumbled out of her mouth, as if she'd been holding them back for too long.

Finally, they were getting somewhere. Lauren repressed the desire to breathe a sigh of relief.

'What do you mean?'

'People thought Finley was great. That he was fun to be with. But when he gambled, he was mean. He stole from me. Money or my possessions so he could sell them. People thought we were close, but we weren't.' Faith's voice was bitter. There were years of resentment evident in her tone.

'Why didn't you tell your parents?' Lauren asked, frowning.

'Because Finley knew about my feelings for Jasmine. He threatened to tell everyone if I told Mum and Dad. So I had to let him do whatever he wanted and keep quiet about it.' Faith's lip curled into a sneer.

'How did Finley find out about you liking Jasmine?' Lauren asked.

'When he was searching my room for money he found some doodles I'd drawn of my name and Jasmine's entwined. He was so smug when he told me what he'd discovered. There was nothing I could do.'

'But you went overseas with him and Jasmine to New Zealand and Australia,' Matt pointed out, frowning in confusion.

Faith nodded, a sad smile playing on her lips. 'To be with Jasmine. To protect her from him.'

'Surely she must have known what he was like. They lived together for their gap year and then more recently at university,' Matt said, sounding sceptical.

'Yeah, well, I think he kept it hidden. But I knew that the moment they were married she would've been unhappy because his real nature would come out. All he ever wanted to do was gamble. Whatever the cost.' Faith's voice rose, the more passionate she became.

'We were under the impression that he'd got over his gambling. Although he owed money, it was from the past and that now he'd stopped,' Lauren interjected, trying to reconcile this new information with what they already knew.

'Of course he hadn't. He never would.' Faith's voice was filled with contempt.

'Did you speak to Jasmine about Finley's gambling?' Lauren asked, keeping her voice neutral.

'Yes, but she wouldn't listen. I tried to explain what he was really like. But she said she could handle him.' Faith's voice was filled with frustration and pain. 'She couldn't. I knew that for sure. I wanted someone better for Jasmine, who would treat her well and not like Finley would have ended up doing.' Faith paused, her eyes glazing over, as if she was seeing something far away.

'Like you?' Lauren asked sensitively. 'Did Jasmine know about your feelings for her?'

Faith nodded, a tear slipping down her cheek. 'Yes. One time when we were out drinking, I let it slip. But she swore not to tell anyone. I didn't want Ruby finding out because she can't keep a secret. I knew it would get out, like it did with how Dylan felt towards Jasmine.'

'Would Dylan have made a good partner for Jasmine?' Matt asked.

Faith's head jerked up. 'No, never.'

'We saw your sketches of him in another notebook. They were dark, to say the least,' Lauren said. 'You must really hate him.'

Faith looked over the top of their heads as if staring at a spot on the wall behind them.

'Answer the DI's question,' Matt said after a few seconds.

'He's a creep. I'd see him staring at Jasmine when she wasn't looking. He didn't deserve her either. No one did.'

'Is that when you decided that if you couldn't have her then no one could?' Lauren asked, taking an educated guess about what had happened.

She looked over at Matt, seeing her own suspicions reflected in his eyes. The air in the room seemed to thicken, and the tension was palpable.

'What are you saying? That I killed them? It wasn't me. Dylan did it. He told me.'

Her words hung ominously in the air for a few seconds, as the three of them took in their implication.

'You told us earlier that he didn't admit to the murder. So why now are you saying he did?' Lauren finally asked.

Faith rested her arms on the table and buried her head. 'I don't know,' she said, her voice muffled. She looked up. 'I was confused. You kept going on about Finley and Jasmine and I'd forgotten that's what he said... Now I've remembered. I'm telling the truth. He did it. Dylan killed them.'

Lauren's phone pinged with a text.

Dylan Fairclough's alibi checks out.

TWENTY-EIGHT
THURSDAY 14 SEPTEMBER

Lauren slid her phone over to Matt so he could see the text and then paused to carefully consider her next move. Should they go along with Faith's assertion that Dylan Fairclough was the killer or confront her straight away? Lauren could sense they were close to the truth, but one wrong step could shut Faith down completely.

'What did you say to Dylan when he admitted to the murders?' Lauren asked, deciding to go along with it for a little while.

'I said he should turn himself in,' Faith replied, sitting up in her chair.

'Did he agree to?' Lauren sat back in her chair, observing the young woman. There had been a subtle change in her facial expression and the way she held herself. It was as if she was acting a part.

'Yes.' Faith nodded.

'Did he agree because he thought you were holding a real gun?'

'Ummm, I don't know. Maybe. Look, I know what I did to Dylan was wrong, but surely you must understand why I did it.

I want to go home now. I'm exhausted. Please may I?' In an exaggerated movement Faith slumped in the chair.

'Sorry, Faith. You won't be going anywhere. Probably for a long time.'

Faith blinked furiously. 'Why?'

'I have to commend you for your acting ability. You're certainly very talented. There's only one thing wrong with your story,' Lauren said, staring directly at her. 'Dylan can't have murdered Jasmine and Finley because he was at home at the time and there are witnesses to this.'

'No. That's wrong,' Faith shouted, both palms on the table and sitting upright. 'I saw him at the beach. He was watching them. He was there, I know it.'

'Yes, we know he was. But he left. But now you've admitted to being there, too, I suggest you tell us the truth. Were you with Jasmine and Finley on the beach the night they got engaged?'

Faith dropped back in her chair, all the fight seeming to drain out of her. 'Yes.'

'Did you drug their prosecco and then murder them?' Lauren asked, struggling to keep her voice steady. She hadn't expected to get a confession so quickly.

'Yes.' Faith's voice was low but in the quiet room, it seemed to echo.

'Why don't you talk us through what you did,' Lauren said, her voice calm despite the anticipation surging through her veins. She leant forward, not wanting to miss a single word.

'Finley showed me the ring he'd bought for Jasmine. He waved it under my nose with a smirk on his face. He knew it would upset me. It was then I decided: if Jasmine couldn't be mine then no one could have her.' Faith stared upwards, as if seeing the scene play out before her.

'But Jasmine hadn't done anything,' Matt exclaimed, his professional demeanour slipping for a moment. 'Did you think of harming your brother and not both of them?'

'No. They both had to go. Jasmine would have known it was me.'

Lauren shivered at the casual way Faith spoke of ending two lives.

'How did you know when and where Finley was going to propose?' Lauren asked.

'Jasmine told me that he wanted to take her somewhere special, so I followed them to the beach and pretended that I was there for a walk and it was a coincidence we had bumped into each other.' Faith's voice was monotone, as if she was reciting a script rather than describing a double murder.

Lauren struggled to keep her voice steady. 'How did you manage to drug them? We didn't find any drugs in your bedroom.'

'The bottle of prosecco and two glasses were in Finley's bedroom on Saturday so I thought he'd be proposing that evening. I took some old sleeping pills from a bottle in the medicine cabinet. They were my mum's. When I saw them on the beach, I congratulated them and offered to take some photos, suggesting they stand closer to the sea. While their backs were turned, I slipped them into the bottle.' Faith's voice was matter-of-fact, as if she was describing a mundane task rather than the prelude to murder.

'Didn't they offer you any?' Lauren asked, wanting to fill in the gaps.

'Yes, Jasmine offered some in her glass but I refused because I was driving.' A flicker of something, regret maybe, or fear, crossed Faith's face before it settled back into its blank mask.

'But the bottle was empty even though they hadn't drunk all of it between them,' Lauren pressed, watching Faith's reaction carefully.

'I tipped the rest of it away behind the rocks.' Faith's voice was flat and emotionless.

'What did you use to suffocate them?' Lauren asked,

wanting to hear it from the young woman, even though they already knew.

'A silk painted cushion.'

'Where did you get it from?' Lauren asked, making sure she sounded unemotional, even though there was horror bubbling inside of her at Faith's calm recitation of events.

'I'd bought one of Alfie's cushions from the exhibition because it was so lovely and decided to use that.' A ghost of a smile played on Faith's lips, and Lauren winced.

'Why did you attend a textile exhibition? How did you even know it was on?' Matt asked.

'I go to all the art exhibitions. And Alfie had mentioned it to me one time when we were talking.'

'Why did you use this particular cushion to murder Jasmine and Finley?' Lauren asked.

'I wanted you to think Alfie might be to blame. To throw you off my trail. Alfie's innocent,' Faith said, her voice dull.

'You can't think much of him if you were prepared to frame him for murder,' Lauren said, with a shake of her head.

'I knew you'd discover it wasn't him eventually. And then you would pin the blame on Dylan.'

'Were you planning to kill Dylan Fairclough?'

'Yes. I wanted you to think he killed Jasmine and Finley and then killed himself because of the guilt.'

'In that case, why did you leave what appeared to be a suicide note?'

'To create a muddle before you eventually worked out that it was Dylan who'd done it.'

'But nothing worked out as planned, did it?' Matt said, shaking his head.

'No.'

'Where's the cushion now?' Lauren asked.

'I burnt it,' Faith replied flatly, her shoulders tensing as she wrapped her arms around herself.

'I see. Faith Glenister, I'm arresting you on suspicion of the murders of Jasmine Dodd and Finley Glenister, and the abduction, with intent to murder, of Dylan Fairclough. You do not have to say anything but it may harm your defence if you do not mention when questioned something which you later rely on in court. Anything you do say may be given in evidence. Do you understand?' Lauren asked.

Faith stared ahead, acting like she hadn't heard the question.

'Do you understand?' Lauren repeated, her voice firm.

'Yes,' Faith muttered, as if all fight had gone out of her.

As Matt ended the recording, Lauren sat back, thoughts careening through her head.

They had their confession, but how many lives had been destroyed in the process?

TWENTY-NINE

THURSDAY 14 SEPTEMBER

Matt headed back into the office, leaving Lauren to inform DCI Mistry of the outcome of the interviews with Faith Glenister and Dylan Fairclough. Though the case was closed, it didn't sit well with him. The senseless loss of two young lives and the devastation left in its wake haunted him. He couldn't shake the image of the shattered families, their worlds forever altered by an act of misguided passion and jealousy.

As he entered the room, he noticed Tamsin sitting next to Ellie on a chair with her bad leg sticking out. The team didn't yet know the outcome of the interviews or that the investigation had come to an end.

'Well, how did it go, Sarge?' Clem asked, his eyes eager for information.

The rest of them paused their work and stared directly at him.

'Faith Glenister has admitted to the murder of Jasmine and Finley. Also, she intended to murder Dylan Fairclough and frame him for the couple's deaths,' he said, sounding matter-of-fact, although his insides were churning.

'Bloody hell. So she actually murdered her brother? That's

crazy,' Billy exclaimed, shaking his head in disbelief. His pen clattered to the desk, forgotten in the shock of the news.

'It turns out that she disliked her brother and loved Jasmine,' Matt explained, stretching his shoulders and attempting to ease the tension. 'She hated Dylan because he loved Jasmine and thought by framing him posthumously it would protect her from being identified as the real murderer.'

'Wow,' Tamsin said, her mouth having dropped open. She shifted in her seat, wincing slightly as she jostled her injured leg. 'I can't believe I've missed all this.' She paused, looking guilty. 'Not that I want there to be more murder cases, obviously.'

Matt sighed. 'She wasn't thinking straight, as far as I can tell.'

He paused, while remembering Faith's broken confession. What could possibly drive someone to kill the person they love? It made no sense to him.

'Does that mean she'll get off, by claiming diminished responsibility, or be charged with manslaughter?' Billy asked.

'I don't know. That's not for us to decide,' Matt said, straightening his shoulders. 'Although it was premeditated so I'm not sure what the Crown Prosecution Service will do. The main thing is that we've done our job.'

'So, case closed?' Billy asked. His eyes darted between Matt and the others, seeking confirmation.

Matt nodded and gave a relieved sigh. 'It certainly looks like it.'

He leant against a nearby desk, the exhaustion of the past few days suddenly catching up with him.

'As long as she doesn't get away with it, that's all I'm concerned about,' Billy said, giving a sharp nod. 'Okay, I get that she wasn't thinking straight, as you said, Sarge, but that doesn't mean she shouldn't pay.'

Matt turned to Tamsin, wanting to change the subject and lighten the mood. 'How are you doing now?'

Tamsin smiled, adjusting her position slightly. 'Fine, thanks, Sarge. My physio's pleased with my progress and I'm ready to come back to work on Monday. Providing I'm behind the desk and not asked to go chasing after criminals. I don't think I'm up to that yet.'

'That I want to see,' Billy said, smirking.

'I promise you'll not be asked to do anything too strenuous,' Matt said, smiling at the officer. He then turned his attention to Ellie. 'Are you excited to be going back to Lenchester?' he asked, trying to keep his voice neutral, even though he knew that he'd miss his friend and colleague when she'd gone.

Ellie's eyes met his briefly before then looking at Billy. 'Yes and no. I'm going to miss everyone here.' She shot a smile at Billy, who beamed back at her.

If someone had told him months ago that Ellie and Billy would be an item, he'd have laughed in their faces. But they were – and made a good couple. He brought Ellie out of herself, and she calmed Billy down.

'But you're going to come and visit, aren't you?' Billy asked, his voice hopeful.

'Of course I am,' Ellie replied warmly. The affection in her voice was clear, and Matt found himself looking away, feeling like an intruder on a private moment.

A twinge of regret ran through Matt that he hadn't had the chance to sit down and discuss the relationship with Ellie. There had never been the time because it had been busy ever since she'd arrived. The dynamics of the team were shifting, and he wondered how it would affect their work going forward.

'Before you leave let's go out for lunch. How about tomorrow?' He wanted to make sure he had a chance to properly say goodbye, and to acknowledge her contribution to the team.

'Yes, that would be lovely,' Ellie said, with a smile.

'What about tonight?' Billy said. 'Surely we're going out to celebrate the end of the case.'

'That's fine, but I can't stay too long,' Matt said. 'Not that you'll miss me. I want to visit my dad.'

Concern flashed across Tamsin's face. 'How's he doing?' she asked, her voice soft with genuine care.

'Oh, he's okay,' Matt said, allowing himself a small smile. 'They're hoping he can come home on Saturday. At least, that's the plan.'

'I'm really pleased for you, Sarge. It can't have been easy juggling the case with him being ill,' Tamsin said, smiling warmly.

'Thanks, Tamsin.' Matt was touched by her support.

'On Saturday night, we're going to have a leaving party for Ellie. Can you come to that, Sarge?' Billy asked, his eyes bright with excitement.

Matt grinned, pushing aside his mixed emotions about Ellie's departure. 'Try and keep me away.'

He clapped his hands together, bringing everyone's attention back to work. 'Sorry to bring the chatter to an end but we've got to tidy up everything, to make sure that the CPS has all the information they need for Faith Glenister's prosecution.' The familiar routine of wrapping up a case grounded him.

'What about Dylan Fairclough?' Clem asked.

'He didn't do anything, and he's already on his way home.' Matt would make sure to check in on Fairclough in a few days, knowing the young man had been through a traumatic experience.

The team dispersed to their tasks and Matt sat down at his desk, his head whirling with the events of the day. He was about to check his emails when Lauren walked into the office and headed over to him.

'The DCI's up to speed, and now we should visit the Glenisters and break the news to them about their daughter. I know it's late but I'd rather they heard it from us and not the media because after the press conference their lives won't be their own.'

THIRTY

THURSDAY 14 SEPTEMBER

The autumn rain drummed steadily against the windscreen as Lauren turned in to the drive of the Glenisters' house.

Matt noted his boss's rigid forearms as she gripped the steering wheel. Breaking news of a murder was one thing. Telling parents their surviving child had killed their other child... that was something else entirely. And then they needed to explain the next steps.

'Ready?' Lauren asked quietly once they'd come to a halt, although they both knew neither of them could ever truly be ready for this.

'Yes, ma'am. At least they're expecting us, so it won't be a surprise.' Before leaving he'd contacted Sonia the FLO to let her know the situation. They had wanted to ensure both parents were there and could be informed at the same time.

'I'll take the lead,' Lauren said, checking her reflection in the rearview mirror.

Matt nodded.

Sonia opened the door before they could ring the bell. 'Hello, ma'am. Sarge. Mr and Mrs Glenister are waiting for you in the drawing room.'

When Lauren and Matt entered the room, Mr Glenister jumped up from where he was sitting beside his wife.

'You've solved it?' Mr Glenister asked, his voice rough with emotion. 'You know who murdered our son. That's why you're here, isn't it?'

'Please sit down,' Lauren said as she sat opposite and Matt did the same.

'Would you like some tea?' Mrs Glenister asked.

'No thank you, we're fine,' Matt said, glancing at Lauren, who he could see was steeling herself for the announcement.

'Mr and Mrs Glenister,' Lauren began, her composure perfect but her eyes full of compassion. 'We've completed our investigation into Finley and Jasmine's deaths and we know exactly what happened that day. The person responsible is now in custody.'

Mrs Glenister leant forward, clutching her husband's hand. 'Thank goodness. Who did it? We need to know.'

Lauren stiffened slightly beside Matt and he heard her take a deep breath.

'It was your daughter, Faith.'

The silence that followed was interminable.

'Faith?' Mrs Glenister whispered. 'Our Faith? No. No. There must be some mistake.'

'I'm so sorry,' Lauren continued gently. 'But the evidence is conclusive and Faith has admitted it.'

Understanding began to dawn in Mr Glenister's eyes. 'Dear God,' he breathed. 'Why?'

'Faith had developed romantic feelings for Jasmine,' Lauren explained. 'But those feelings weren't reciprocated. She'd also become convinced that Finley wasn't good enough for Jasmine. The engagement was the final straw and that's why she decided to do what she did.'

Mr Glenister glanced at his wife. 'The way she looked at that girl. We did notice, didn't we? But we thought... we thought

Faith was jealous of their relationship because she wasn't seeing anyone. We had no idea that...' His words fell away.

Mrs Glenister, her face ashen, stared at Lauren and Matt. 'I don't understand. Faith seemed as devastated as we were. We cried together. Talked about Finley together. She even helped us pick out his coffin. And yet all the time—' Her voice broke.

'What happens now?' Mr Glenister asked.

'The evidence will go to the Crown Prosecution Service and they'll get back to us regarding the charges. You'll need to find her some legal representation.'

'Yes of course...' He paused, wiping the tears from his eyes. 'Can we see her?' he asked, but was looking at his wife, as if seeking confirmation that's what they wanted.

'I'm afraid not. But we will need both of you to come to station to make a statement over the next day or so.'

Mr Glenister nodded and then sank into the sofa. 'Both of them,' he murmured. 'We've lost both our children. One to death and one to—' He couldn't finish.

Lauren leant forward slightly, her hands clutched together. 'I know nothing we say can soften the blow of such an awful situation. But Sonia will support you through the process. There are also several excellent counselling services in Cornwall that specialise in—'

'No,' Mrs Glenister interrupted, her voice suddenly sharp. 'We want to be alone. Please will you leave us.'

Matt and Lauren exchanged a loaded look. The Glenisters weren't going to like what Lauren was about to tell them.

'We sympathise with how you must be feeling,' Lauren said. 'But unfortunately it's not that simple because we require forensics to go through Faith's bedroom and the rest of the house.'

'Why?' Mrs Glenister demanded.

'Faith's room, and by default the rest of the house, is now a potential crime scene.

We're very sorry about this, but it's procedure and can't be changed. I've arranged for forensics to arrive a little later. I wanted time to explain everything to you. Is there anywhere you can stay while the house is out of bounds?' Lauren asked. 'You can take some belongings with you.'

'My wife's sister lives in Lamorna. We can go there,' Mr Glenister said. 'I'll message her now.'

'Thank you. We'll leave you for now. Sonia will help with anything you need.'

As they walked back to the car, leaving the Glenisters to grapple with the cruel truth that had taken both their children in very different ways, Matt heard the first seagulls of the evening wheeling overhead, their cries carrying on the salt wind from the harbour. It was as if they were oblivious to the tragedy going on beneath them.

Lauren paused before opening the car door. 'I hope I never have to do that again. We've destroyed the lives of those people and I doubt they'll ever recover.'

'We were simply the messengers. At least they heard the truth from us, not whatever twisted version the papers will run tomorrow,' Matt said.

'You're right, of course. But it still wasn't easy.'

Matt nodded, understanding completely. They'd watched a family confront a second devastating loss – not to death this time, but to something that might be even harder to bear.

THIRTY-ONE
THURSDAY 14 SEPTEMBER

When Matt returned to the office, he was surprised to see Tamsin staring intently at Ellie's computer screen. He headed over to them.

'Still here?' he said to Tamsin.

'Yes, Ellie's catching me up with everything. You don't mind, do you?' Tamsin replied.

'Of course not. It will be strange on Monday after being off for so long, so this will help.'

Billy headed over to them, a mischievous grin on his face. 'Hey, Sarge, now that the case is closed, fancy sharing any office gossip you've been holding back?'

Matt raised an eyebrow. 'Why would you think I've got gossip to share? I'm shocked you'd even suggest such a thing, Billy.'

Clem chuckled from his desk. 'The only gossip around here is how many biscuits you manage to sneak from the packet left in the kitchen, Billy.'

'Oi,' Billy protested, but his grin widened. 'I'll have you know I'm on a strict diet of... oh, who am I kidding? I can't keep away from them.'

Ellie rolled her eyes fondly. 'And I thought I was dating a health nut.'

'Health nut?' Tamsin snorted. 'More like a junk-food squirrel.'

The office erupted in laughter, the tension from the case dissipating in the warm camaraderie.

Matt shook his head, smiling. 'All right, you lot. Less chatting, more working. We still need to get the case details to the CPS as soon as possible.'

'Yes, sir,' Billy said, giving a mock salute before heading back to his desk.

As the afternoon wore on, the banter continued intermittently, punctuating the sound of typing and phone calls.

'Hey, Ellie,' Clem called out during a lull. 'What's the first thing you're going to do when you get back to Lenchester?'

Ellie thought for a moment. 'Go for a curry at The Royal Bengal restaurant. I've missed their tikka masala.'

'Ooh, curry.' Billy perked up. 'Do you think they'd deliver to Penzance?'

'In your dreams, mate.' Tamsin laughed. 'Though I wouldn't say no to a good curry myself. Maybe we should make that our leaving do for Ellie?'

Matt nodded, warming to the idea. 'Not a bad call, Tamsin. What do you think, Ellie? A curry for your send-off?'

'Sounds perfect,' Ellie agreed, her smile tinged with a hint of sadness.

'Right then, curry it is,' Billy said. 'We'll meet at the pub first and make a night of it. We can celebrate solving cases and clogged arteries.'

'Billy,' Ellie admonished, but she was laughing along with everyone else.

After thirty minutes Matt stood up and stretched his tired muscles. 'I'm done for the day. Let's go for a quick drink to celebrate solving the case. I'll go and let the DI know.'

Once he returned from Lauren's office, the team started packing up, the office filled with the sounds of drawers closing and computers shutting down.

'First round's on me,' Clem offered.

'In that case, I'm ordering the most expensive thing on the menu,' Billy quipped.

'It's a pub, Billy, not a Michelin-star restaurant,' Tamsin retorted. 'We're having a drink.'

As they filed out, Matt hung back, catching Ellie's eye. He motioned her over, feeling the need to have a few words.

'Listen, Ellie,' he said quietly, 'I know things have been hectic, but I wanted to say, I'm really happy for you and Billy. And I'm going to miss having you on the team.'

Ellie smiled, a hint of sadness in her eyes. 'Thanks, Matt. I'm going to miss being here too. But you know, Lenchester isn't that far. I'll be back to visit.'

Matt nodded, forcing a smile. 'I know you will. And hey, maybe I'll even make it up there sometime.'

'I hope so. Does that mean lunch tomorrow is off?' Ellie asked with a slight frown.

'No. But we'll be off site then and I didn't want to talk work.'

Ellie walked away to join Billy and Matt took a deep breath, the drama of the day suddenly catching up with him.

He'd have a quick drink and then head to visit his father. Hopefully they'd get the confirmation they were all hoping for: that he could come home.

THIRTY-TWO

SATURDAY 16 SEPTEMBER

Matt stood by the window in the lounge of his parents' house, his eyes scanning the quiet street outside. The constant rain had finally given way to some weak sunshine and the anticipation of his dad's return was building – although he'd be lying if he didn't admit to being worried about his future.

'Are they here yet?' Dani asked impatiently, standing next to him on her tiptoes. Her small hands were pressed against the glass, leaving smudges that Matt would normally rush to clean. Today, he couldn't bring himself to care.

Matt smiled at his daughter's enthusiasm, a surge of love for her coursing through him. 'I can see the car coming down the street,' he said, placing a hand on Dani's shoulder. He could feel her vibrating with excitement under his touch. 'But I don't want you jumping all over Grandpa when he comes inside. He hasn't been well, remember?'

Dani nodded solemnly, clutching a piece of paper in her hands. The edges were slightly crumpled from her grip. 'I know that. I want to give him my get-well card that I made with Grandma.'

'I'm sure he's going to love it.' Matt ran a hand over his daughter's hair, smoothing down the flyaway strands.

The sound of the car pulling up outside, and reversing into a parking space, made them both turn. Matt's heart rate picked up as he heard car doors slamming shut.

The door opened, and Dani burst out, unable to contain her excitement. 'Grandpa. Grandpa!' she called, her voice ringing out in the quiet street.

'Hello, little one,' Matt's dad replied, his voice warm but tired.

'Where's Grandma?' Dani asked.

'She's bringing my things inside.'

Matt held open the door as his mum – loaded with a small suitcase and a pillow that she'd taken to the hospital – rushed up to the front door. He turned to his dad, who was bending down slightly to greet Dani. His movements were stiff.

'Let's go into the lounge,' Matt suggested, while studying his dad carefully.

He looked okay, just very tired. The hospital stay had left its mark. There were dark circles under his eyes, and his clothes seemed to hang a bit looser on his frame, despite him being in there less than a week.

'That's a good idea,' Matt's mum said. 'You all go into the lounge, and I'll make us a cup of tea.'

'I'll come with you, Mum,' Matt added, sensing his mother might need a moment to talk. He caught her eye, noting the weariness and worry etched on her face.

'I'll look after Grandpa,' Dani said, holding up the colourful card she'd made. 'I've made you a special card.'

'Thank you, princess,' Matt's father said, his face softening as he and Dani sat down on the sofa. Matt watched his father wincing slightly as he lowered himself onto the cushions, all the time trying to hide his discomfort from his granddaughter.

Matt walked into the kitchen with his mum, his head full of questions and concerns. The familiar space felt different somehow, as if the worry of the past few days had seeped into the walls. Once they were alone, he turned to her. 'He's looking okay. What did the doctors say? I didn't want to ask in front of him.'

His mother sighed and leant back against the work top. The overhead light cast shadows on her face, emphasising the lines of worry. 'They've said that we're to take this as a warning. He's got to take it easy for the next little while. He's got some pills to take on a regular basis to keep his blood pressure down. That's it really. I'm not sure I understood everything they said – all those long words. But we've got to see our doctor and I'll ask him to explain it to me.'

Matt nodded, processing the information. He began mechanically preparing the tea, the familiar routine helping to calm his nerves. 'Did they say how long it will be until Dad is back to normal?'

'We'll have a new normal,' his mother replied, her voice heavy with resignation. 'We're going to be eating well and he's going to take plenty of exercise. There's to be no stress and strain from now on.'

Matt took a deep breath. It was time to bring up the idea he'd been contemplating. 'I've been thinking, Mum, and I don't want you to say no because I think it's a good idea.' He paused, gathering his thoughts. The kettle boiled furiously, filling the silence. 'I'm going to look into buying a property around here. I think Dad needs the peace and quiet, and Dani needs more space so she can charge around.'

'But—' his mum started to protest, stopping when Matt held up a hand. He could see the conflict in her eyes. She was torn between wanting to keep the family close and recognising the need for change.

'But nothing, Mum. I think it's for the best. You know, there's a house down the road that's up for sale. If I buy it, we'll be very close and we can still do everything together. You can have Dani like you do now, and take her to nursery. I was thinking that now she's a bit older, it would be good for her to go more often.' The kitchen suddenly felt too small with the weight of the decision pressing down on them. 'And I'll still be around to help you with Dad.'

'Yes, I know that, love,' his mother said, her voice soft. She busied herself with arranging biscuits on a plate, although her hands were shaking. 'But still...'

'I think you'll enjoy having a bit of peace and quiet. You know yourself that we're so cramped in this place, and if anyone wants to come and stay, it's impossible.'

'Well, I suppose it could work.'

Matt nodded, a sense of relief washing over him, because his mum was actually considering the idea.

'I think it will be good for you and Dad to have more time to yourselves.'

'But you know we'll look after Dani at any time.'

'Yes, of course I know that,' Matt replied. 'Especially when I'm working late.'

'And you might like some privacy, too. You know, if ever you want to bring someone home,' his mum said, with a wink.

'Maybe,' he said, dismissing her with a wave of his hand. No way was he ready for anything like that. Not yet. He couldn't do that to Leigh's memory.

His mother was quiet for a moment, then nodded slowly. 'You know what? Your idea is a good one. But don't tell your dad yet because he'll think it's all due to him being sick and we don't want that weighing on his mind.'

'Agreed. I'm going to have a look at the house and you can come with me if you like. If we both think it's right for me and Dani, I'll put in an offer.'

'Perfect. Now what time are you heading out?' his mum

asked, changing the subject. 'You've got Ellie's farewell party, haven't you?'

A twinge of sadness hit him at the thought of Ellie leaving. The kitchen suddenly felt too warm, too confining. 'I'm leaving around seven.'

His mother gave him a knowing look. 'You're going to miss her, aren't you?'

'Yes. And I'm not the only one,' he said with a smile.

'What do you mean?' his mother asked.

'She's struck up a relationship with Billy.'

'What, Billy? The one that you've often talked about? The one that's a bit...?' his mother trailed off, raising an eyebrow.

Matt chuckled. 'Oh, Billy's fine now. Especially since being with Ellie. It's an odd combination, but I think she's good for him. She's certainly calmed him down a bit.' He paused. 'We're all going to miss Ellie. She's been a fantastic addition to the team.'

'But you've got the other officer coming back, haven't you?'

'Tamsin. We're all looking forward to her return to work. She's also a good member of the team.'

While finishing preparing the tea, Matt allowed his mind to wander. He thought about the potential new house, imagining Dani running around a larger garden, and his parents relaxing in a quieter space. He also thought about his father's health and the adjustments they'd need to make. The new routines they'd have to establish. And then he thought about Ellie, leaving for Lenchester, and how Billy was going to cope.

Life kept moving forward whether they were ready or not.

Carrying the tray of tea into the lounge, Matt smiled at the scene in front of him. His father was listening intently to Dani, who was explaining her card in great detail, and she'd snuggled up to him, her small hand patting his arm gently. While at the same time his mother fussed with cushions and blankets, making sure everyone was comfortable. It warmed Matt's heart, reminding him of what was truly important.

Settling into a chair and balancing his teacup, Matt made a silent promise to himself. He'd make these changes work. For his parents. For Dani. And for himself. He owed it to Leigh, who he often sensed was close by, looking down on them.

Whatever changes lay ahead, whatever challenges they might face, they'd face them together. And that, he realised, was all that really mattered.

THIRTY-THREE

SATURDAY 16 SEPTEMBER

Lauren pushed open the heavy wooden door of The Crown, the familiar scent of beer and pub food hitting her nostrils. The noise of laughter and chatter swept over her as she stepped inside, a stark contrast to the quiet evening outside. She paused for a moment, letting her eyes adjust to the dimly lit interior.

The pub was bustling with Saturday night energy. Every table seemed to be occupied, and the bar was three deep with people jostling to be served. Lauren cast an eye over the room, looking for her team. She'd been debating how long to stay at Ellie's leaving celebration because she didn't want to get in the way. Maybe she'd stay for a drink but not go for the curry. The team probably wouldn't want her hanging around anyway.

Finally, she spotted them at a large round table in the corner. Matt, Billy, Ellie, Tamsin, Clem and Jenna. All of them were laughing, probably at something Billy had said, knowing him. His hands were gesticulating wildly and his face was animated as he regaled the group with some tale.

Lauren took a deep breath, smoothed down her shirt, and headed over with a smile. As she approached, she caught the tail end of the story.

'... and then the suspect says, "Well, Officer, if I knew it was illegal, I wouldn't have done it in front of the police station,"' Billy finished with a flourish.

The group erupted into laughter, and Clem nearly choked on his pint. Matt was shaking his head, a grin plastered on his face.

'Who wants a drink?' Lauren said, trying to inject some enthusiasm into her voice. She felt slightly out of place and that she was intruding on their fun.

A chorus of orders came her way, accompanied by grateful smiles. She took a mental note of each request, nodding as she did so.

'I'll help you, ma'am,' Billy said, jumping up eagerly. His chair scraped loudly against the floor, drawing a few looks from nearby tables.

They made their way to the bar, weaving through the crowd until they were behind several other people waiting to be served.

'You'll miss Ellie, won't you?' Lauren said, glancing sideways at Billy as they waited. She'd already noticed how his eyes kept darting back to the table where Ellie sat.

'Yes, ma'am, I will,' Billy replied, his usual animated face softening. There was a vulnerability in his expression that Lauren rarely saw.

Lauren hesitated, then decided to press on. 'Is it serious between the two of you?' She immediately backtracked, 'Oh, sorry, I shouldn't really ask, I—'

'No, it's fine. You can ask, ma'am,' Billy interrupted, smiling. 'Ellie's very different from any other girl I've dated. We're going to see if we can make it work. I can go to Lenchester to see her and she can come down here sometimes.'

Lauren nodded, surprised by Billy's openness. 'Have you ever visited Lenchester before?'

'No, but I'm looking forward to going there. To see the *real* murder capital of the country,' Billy said with a grin. 'Although, having said that, we're fast catching up.'

Lauren frowned, her professional instincts kicking in. 'Don't say that, Billy,' she said firmly. 'We don't want to be compared with them. We're too small a team to have to deal with murder after murder.'

Billy's grin faded slightly. 'I think it's a bit late for that, ma'am. Now we've got Sarge working here. He seems to have brought the murder vibe with him. Not that I'm complaining, because it beats sorting out graffiti.'

The man behind the bar came over, and Lauren gave their drinks order, her mind churning over Billy's words. Was he right? Had Matt really brought all the murders with him? No, that was ridiculous. It didn't work that way. She pushed the thought aside.

'It will be nice for you to visit the big city,' she said, forcing a lighter tone. 'And maybe Ellie will show you around the station, so you can see what it's like to work in such an environment.'

'Yes, but I'm happy here. You know that,' Billy said, his voice serious. 'At one time I thought I'd like to leave for a more exciting force, but not now. This is my home and I like it here.' He chuckled. 'I must've been hanging around with Clem for too long. I'm sounding old before my time.'

After paying for the drinks, they headed back to the table. It was strange that Billy had confided in her, especially as in the past they'd had a rocky relationship: mainly because she'd wanted him to conform more. But now she was more relaxed about his behaviour and appreciated him for who he was. Ellie had certainly been a good influence on him. Hopefully it would continue when the two were living so far apart.

Once the drinks had been distributed and Lauren and Billy had sat down, Tamsin raised her glass. 'I'd like to make a toast to me starting work on Monday, and Ellie, thank you for every-thing. You've been a great roommate, and I'm going to miss you.'

'We're going to miss you at work, too,' Jenna added, her eyes slightly misty.

'Thank you,' Ellie said, blushing slightly. 'I'm going to miss you, too.'

'Especially me,' Billy said, waving his arms and nearly knocking over his drink in the process.

'*Especially* you, Billy,' Ellie said with a smile, her eyes soft as she looked at him.

'And Matt – Sarge,' Billy added hastily, realising his slip.

'Yes, and Matt,' Ellie said.

Lauren was about to add to Tamsin's words when her phone rang. Seeing the number, she frowned. The cheerful atmosphere of the pub had suddenly become distant and unreal.

'Sorry, I've got to get this,' she said, hurriedly leaving the table.

She answered the phone while moving to a quiet corner of the pub. The sounds of laughter and clinking glasses faded into the background as she pressed the phone to her ear.

'Lauren speaking.'

'Sorry to bother you, Lauren,' her aunt Julia said, her voice shaky. 'Something's happened and you were the only person I could think of to call.'

Shock surged through Lauren's body as she listened to her aunt explain what had happened, and the pub's warm atmosphere turned stifling. This wasn't something Lauren could ignore. She had to act straight away. At the end of the call, she returned to the table and caught Matt's eye. She nodded for him to follow her over to a table close by.

The others were too busy laughing at another of Billy's jokes and didn't notice the pair of them leave.

'What's the matter, ma'am?' Matt asked as they sat down, his face etched with concern.

Lauren dragged in a deep breath, while still reeling from the news. The sounds of the pub seemed to fade away, leaving only the pounding of her heart in her ears. 'I've got to go and can't stay for the curry. Something's come up which I have to deal with straight away.'

'What is it?' Matt pressed gently, his eyes searching her face.

Lauren paused, the weight of the words she was about to say pressing down on her. 'My aunt Julia has been arrested for the murder of my uncle Roy.'

Matt's eyebrows shot up, his face paling. 'Did she do it?' he asked, his voice thick with shock.

'I don't know.' The enormity of the situation began to sink in, and a cold dread settled over her. 'She used her only phone call to contact me. I've got to arrange for a solicitor, but first I want to see her. She's at Bodmin station.'

'Would you like me to come with you?' Matt offered, already half-rising from his seat.

His loyalty touched her, even in this moment of crisis.

Lauren shook her head, knowing she had to handle this alone. 'Thanks for offering, I appreciate it more than you know. But it's not necessary. You stay here and enjoy the party. This is going to be a long process.' Her voice trembled slightly, betraying her inner turmoil.

Matt sat back down, his brow furrowed. 'Is it something she could have done?' he asked, his voice barely audible over the pub's noise.

'I didn't ask, but I wouldn't blame her if she did. He's given her hell over the years, emotionally and physically. If she is guilty, then I certainly hope there are mitigating circumstances.' She stood up. 'Go and enjoy the party. Please tell the team that something's come up. But don't say what.'

'Of course, I won't,' Matt reassured her.

'Thanks. Could you please tell Ellie goodbye from me and remind her to keep in touch?'

'Will do, ma'am,' Matt said, still looking worried. 'I'll see you on Monday, but if you need anything before then, let me know. I'm around all weekend.'

'Thanks, Matt,' Lauren said, managing a small smile. 'But you have your dad to take care of. How is he?'

'He's good. It's better now he's home. Anyway, remember, I'm here for you.'

'Thanks. This isn't going to be an easy situation to deal with.'

The understatement of her words hung in the air between them.

Lauren made her way through the pub, a kaleidoscope of thoughts messing with her head. The celebratory atmosphere of moments ago felt like a distant memory, replaced by a sense of uncertainty. Now, she faced difficult conversations and legal complications. And just when she thought things were quietening down.

But she owed it to her aunt – the only person who had really cared about Lauren since her parents had died.

Lauren stepped out into the cool night air and squared her shoulders.

Whatever challenges arose, she'd face them head-on, as she always did. Her aunt needed her, and that was where she had to be. The detective in her was already analysing the situation, but the niece in her was determined to be there no matter what. She thought of Matt's words: 'I'm here for you.' It was a small comfort, but helped.

Lauren was determined to find a way through this, for herself and for her aunt.

Whatever lay ahead, she was ready to face it, one step at a time.

A LETTER FROM THE AUTHOR

Dear reader,

Huge thanks for reading *Death at Porthcurno Cove*. I hope you enjoyed returning to Lauren and Matt's world once again for this new case. If you want to join other readers in hearing all about my new books, you can sign up here:

www.stormpublishing.co/sally-rigby

If you enjoyed the book and could spare a few moments to leave a review that would be hugely appreciated. Even a short review can make all the difference in encouraging a reader to discover my books for the first time. Thank you so much!

I loved writing this book because of it being set in Porthcurno, which is one of my favourite parts of Cornwall, and somewhere I've visited many times over the last thirty years. I also found fascinating exploring how obsession can lead to the ultimate betrayal.

Thanks again for being part of this amazing journey with me and I hope you'll stay in touch – I have so many more stories and ideas to entertain you with!

Sally Rigby

KEEP IN TOUCH WITH THE AUTHOR

For a free novella and exclusive bonus content,
visit: www.sallyrigby.com

facebook.com/Sally-Rigby-1314146305 27848
instagram.com/sally.rigby.author

ACKNOWLEDGEMENTS

First, I'd like to express thanks to my incredible advance reader team who once again helped me get this book right. If it wasn't for them, I suspect most readers would have guessed who did it very early on indeed.

To my brilliant editors, Claire Bord and Kathryn Taussig – thanks for your expertise, and insightfulness. I never cease to be amazed how you manage to turn what I submit into something so much better.

Thanks to everyone at Storm Publishing, from editorial staff, to cover designers, and sales and marketing. Without you this book simply wouldn't exist.

A special thank you to my sister-in-law, Jacqui, whose knowledge of the area and hospitality when I visit has been invaluable.

Finally, thanks to my family for always being there for me.

Printed in Great Britain
by Amazon